The Last of the OG's

Tranay Adams

Lock Down Publications and Ca$h Presents
The Last of the OG's
A Novel by *Tranay Adams*

Tranay Adams

Lock Down Publications
P.O. Box 944
Stockbridge, Ga 30281
www.lockdownpublications.com

Copyright 2021 Tranay Adams
The Last of the OG's

Lock Down Publications
Like our page on Facebook: Lock Down Publications @
www.facebook.com/lockdownpublications.ldp
Cover design and layout by: **Dynasty Cover Me**
Book interior design by: **Shawn Walker**
Edited by: **Tamira Butler**

Stay Connected with Us!

Text **LOCKDOWN** to 22828 to stay up-to-date with new releases, sneak peaks, contests and more...

Thank you!

Submission Guideline.

Submit the first three chapters of your completed manuscript to ldpsubmissions@gmail.com, subject line: Your book's title. The manuscript must be in a .doc file and sent as an attachment. Document should be in Times New Roman, double spaced and in size 12 font. Also, provide your synopsis and full contact information. If sending multiple submissions, they must each be in a separate email.

Have a story but no way to send it electronically? You can still submit to LDP/Ca$h Presents. Send in the first three chapters, written or typed, of your completed manuscript to:

LDP: Submissions Dept
P.O. Box 944
Stockbridge, Ga 30281

DO NOT send original manuscript. Must be a duplicate.

Provide your synopsis and a cover letter containing your full contact information.

Thanks for considering LDP and Ca$h Presents.

Acknowledgements

Jane Pennella, Dorothea Creamer, Tanya Garry, Helene Young, Lulee Kitty, LeShe Beckham, Eliza Tellis, Juanita Taylor, T.J. Edwards, Jelissa Edwards, and Jeannette Frazier.

Tranay Adams

Chapter One
2000

Although it was dark out, the scattered stars and the full moon shone in the sky marvelously. The occasional gust of wind disturbed the loose trash on the ground and tickled the leaves of the trees. A homeless woman in dirty, tattered clothing sifted through garbage for recyclables while stray dogs wandered aimlessly, snooping around for discarded food. This was a normal night in downtown China Town. There wasn't anything happening out of the ordinary that looked suspicious. Not even to the three shady-looking characters in a parked SUV, looking to make a score that could get them a lifetime behind bars.

Hitt-Man sat behind the wheel of a white Escalade truck on stock rims. His attention was focused out of the driver's window at the Chinese restaurant, and he was drumming his fingers on the steering wheel. Occasionally, he'd glance at his gold Presidential Rolex. He was accompanying his boss, Caleb, to a dope deal. They were supposed to have been there at seven o'clock, but his employer liked to be at places earlier. So, they'd gotten there ahead of time and had a twenty-minute wait before they could head on over.

Out the corner of his eye, Hitt-Man could see Brad scratching underneath his chin and the inside of his track-marked arm. He frowned, thinking how much the white boy's scratching reminded him of a flea-bitten dog. He understood that Brad was a dopehead and he was fiending to get his medicine. But still, all that goddamn scratching was driving Hitt-Man's ass up the wall.

"My nigga, do you really gotta scratch like that? I'm starting to itch watching yo' ass," Hitt-Man stated with a disgusted look plastered on his face. One hand held the steering wheel while the other held a blue-raspberry Tootsie Roll sucker.

Hitt-Man was a six-foot-one, dark-skinned nigga with a body builder's physique. He had shoulder-length locs that were styled in plaits, and a goatee. He wore six gold rope chains around his neck. Each one was bigger than the last. The last and biggest rope had a bust of Nefertiti hanging from it. In addition to the gold ropes, he had on two four-finger rings on each hand. The first four-finger ring spelled "Hitt," and the second four-finger ring spelled "Man."

Hitt-Man was Caleb's bodyguard and enforcer. Their friendship went way back to the 10th grade. He was the new Haitian kid in school who spoke broken English and dressed in hand-me-down clothes. Caleb, on the other hand, thanks to drug money, stayed in the latest drip and jewelry. He rolled a milk-white '93 BMW 325i and had his own apartment. One day, he caught a couple of kids bullying Hitt-Man for his accent and raggedy attire. Hitt-Man gave the kids a beating so bad that an ambulance had to come get them. Despite being the one that was being harassed, Hitt-Man wound up with a three-day suspension. Impressed by the way he'd handled the knuckleheads at school, Caleb offered Hitt-Man a job as his muscle, and he took it. Ever since then, the two of them had been inseparable. Wherever Caleb went, Hitt-Man was there following him like his shadow. His reputation grew with his physical size and the lethal force he used to handle Caleb's adversaries.

"My bad, Hitt, I needa get right," Brad told him. "You know how it is when a fiend hasn't had his or her fix." He continued to his chest, which caused Hitt-Man to start scratching as well. Dopefiend Brad was wearing shades at the top of his head, a sleeveless denim jean jacket, and flip flops. A pouch secured to the loops of his denim jean shorts housed all the items he needed to shoot his dope with.

"No, the fuck I don't know how it is. I'm notta fucking dopefiend," Hitt-Man told him. "Only thang I fiend for is money and pussy—lots of both. Me and you are not the same, white boy."

"Yeah, whatever," Brad replied then glanced in the sun-visor's mirror at Caleb. "Yo, Cal, man, how much longer we got before it's time to holla at these tight eyes?"

Brad's name wasn't legally Brad. It was actually Cyril, but niggaz in the hood had a difficult time pronouncing it. They were straightup butchering his shit! Since he just so happened to be one of the only white faces in the ghetto, they decided to nickname him, Brad. He wasn't feeling it at first, but eventually, it grew on him. In fact, it grew on him so much, he decided to only go by the name Brad.

"That's a good question, Brad, lemme see," Caleb re-plied from the backseat where he was reading an article in *Forbes* magazine and sipping a cup of 7-11 coffee. He sat his cup inside of the holder and glanced at his sophisticated timepiece. "Hell, we've got two more minutes. That lil' time will be gone once we make it across the street. Let's roll." He sat the magazine aside and waited for Hitt-Man to open his door.

Caleb was a light-skinned nigga with freckles sprinkled over his face. He had steel-gray eyes and an auburn beard. He stood six-feet tall and had a stocky physique. Although he was waist deep in the drug game, Caleb didn't dress flashy, and he wasn't as flamboyant as his peers in the same profession. In fact, the nigga dressed more like a college professor, with his eyeglasses, turtleneck, and blazer. If you were to see homeboy in traffic, you'd swear to God Al-mighty he was on his way to work at a university to teach a class. But looks were most definitely deceiving, because he was the other side of a silver-dollar coin.

Caleb's parents were just teenagers when they gave his grandmother full custody of him. Mrs. Barbara Sheryl had raised him to be a well-mannered, God-fearing, hard-working boy. And as far as she could see, he'd become just that. Well, at least that's what he was when he was around her and the other folks they attended church with. But as soon as Caleb was out of the old hen's eyesight, he was out in the streets breaking bad and running afoul of the law. The young man took to hanging with a far older group of knuckleheads, smoking, drinking, and committing petty crimes. Eventually, the wildlings took their game of mischief to another level when they started burglarizing Asian families' houses and jacking cars to sell to chop shops. From there, the resident junkie, BoBo, introduced them to his drug of choice, heroin.

BoBo taught Caleb and his ragtag crew everything he knew about Boy (another word for dope) for the very low price of a ten-dollar bag of it, of course. Now, while his crew had grown disinterested with the old vagabond's lessons, Caleb became intrigued and wanted to know more. He wanted to capitalize on the knowledge that BoBo was giving him, so over the course of a week, he'd pay in the form of ten-dollar bags of dope. Confident that he could hustle the shit himself, Caleb paid BoBo to introduce him to a plug he knew and to show him how to cut the shit. Caleb stacked up all the loot from the capers he and his crew went on and went to cop from the plug. Once the fiends had gotten a taste of the young nigga's dope, the hood went into a frenzy, like sharks when a drop of blood was in their surrounding waters.

The money was flowing in so good, the crew couldn't help but take notice. They wanted in on the new hustle their comrade had found. Caleb, never having been a greedy nigga, brought them in so they could eat right alongside him. He didn't have any problem with breaking bread with his niggaz. The way he saw it, there was plenty of paper to spread around, so there wasn't any need for him to be stingy.

Unfortunately for Caleb, his plug and his partner got knocked off by a rival cartel in Mexico, so he had to scramble to find someone else. Luckily for him, he kept the telephone number of an acquaintance of his he'd met through mutual friends: Wang Lie. Now, Wang Lie wasn't exactly the plug. He was the man next to the man who was said to have some of the best dog food (heroin) since Alpo. Needless to say, Caleb didn't waste any time setting up a meeting with Wang so he could possibly get his hands on some work. Less than forty-eight hours later, here he and the men he'd assembled were.

As soon as Hitt-Man opened the back door, Caleb stepped out of the whip, one 500-dollar leather dress shoe at a time. Once the door was closed behind him, he buttoned up his jacket and took in his surroundings. Brad came to stand beside him.

Once Hitt-Man finished his sucker, he tossed the stick aside and escorted his boss and the fiend across the street. He kept a close eye on things as they crossed the somewhat busy street. Both of his hands were ready to draw his guns and get it popping, if need be.

Caleb, Hitt-Man, and Brad were stopped at the entrance of the restaurant by a Chinaman as tall as Shaq. He had tattooed hands as well as a tattooed goatee. His long, silky, jet-black hair was pulled back into a ponytail. He was wearing a powder-blue turtleneck underneath a black sports coat and slacks. The only piece of jewelry he had on was a beaded black bracelet with gold Chinese writing on each of the beads.

"I'm gonna have to pat you guys down before you enter," the tall Chinaman told them.

"The only one strapped is me, big dog," Hitt-Man said and flashed him the guns in his shoulder holsters.

"No one enters through these doors packing," the tall Chinaman said and held out his hand. "Hand 'em over and you'll get 'em back once you leave."

"You must be out cho noodle-eating mind." Hitt-Man's face balled with hostility. "I'm not going inside those doors naked while y'all yellow asses are packing heat. Fuck I look like, a fool?"

"The biggest one I've ever seen," the tall Chinaman replied angrily. He wanted to slam his fist on top of Hitt-Man's head and crush his skull.

Hitt-Man stepped before the tall Chinaman and looked up at him. It was like he was mad dogging a twenty-foot-tall tree. He only reached the giant's belt buckle.

"You insult me again, and you and I are gonna make an action movie," Hitt-Man swore as he pulled his guns from their holsters and cocked the hammers on them. He held them down at his sides, but the moment the giant made a move, he was going to soak that ass up!

The Chinaman clenched his teeth and balled his fists so tight that the veins riddling them bulged. He was going to kick Hitt-Man dead in his chest and shoot him in the face. Right when he was about to make his move, someone spoke to him through his earbud. The anger disappeared from his face as he pressed the bud further into his ear and listened closely.

"Yes, sir, they're here," the Chinaman reported, looking over Caleb and them. "Yes, I understand, Mr. Lei." He

14

cleared his throat with his fist to his mouth. "I apologize for the inconvenience I may have caused. I just got word from Mr. Lei. He says you're to enter with your weapons."

Hitt-Man looked his tall ass up and down. "Your boss just saved your ass, Yoa Ming." He holstered his firearms and watched as the tall Chinaman opened the restaurant door for them to enter. He could tell by the expression on his face that he was fighting back the urge to say something slick back to him.

Hitt-Man, Caleb, and Brad fell in step inside of the restaurant. They took in the scenery as they stood at the center of the establishment. There was a big gold statue of a dragon in the middle of the room. The walls were covered in red, black, and gold Chinese calligraphy. Red, black, and gold Chinese lanterns hung from the ceiling. The tables placed throughout the restaurant were covered with red and gold tablecloths. A vase covered with Chinese artwork and filled with colorful flowers sat upon each table. The restaurant had two levels. The upper level had a black wooden guardrail, and it was covered by red and gold sheer curtains. The Chinese archway, which was on the opposite side of the gold dragon tattoo, was the path to the men's and women's restrooms. A sign hung from the archway. Written in Chinese letters were men and women's restrooms with arrows pointing in the direction where each one was located.

Caleb, Hitt-Man, and Brad were amazed by the décor of the restaurant. Brad even went so far as to rub on the gold dragon. Hitt-Man scowled and smacked the shit out the back of Brad's neck. Brad's face balled from the stinging sensation, and he grabbed the back of his aching neck. He turned around to Hitt-Man, looking at him like he'd lost his goddamn mind.

"Say, bro, what the fuck is yo' problem?" Brad asked. He looked like he wanted to fight Hitt-Man, but he knew better. He couldn't see the muscle-bound brute with the hands or the guns.

"I already know what chu thinking, white boy," Hitt-Man said with his upper lip pulled back in a sneer. "You notta 'bouta grab some of your dopehead buddies and come back to steal this statue."

"Man, you're tripping, Hitt-Man, I wasn't thinking about stealing this big ass statue," Brad told him convincingly. He was trying to see if the statue was real gold because he had every intention of stealing that mothafucka. The moment he laid eyes on the dragon, he was thinking of how much money he could sell it for. Whatever money he got for it, it would be all profit. And he was going to use that shit to get as high as a kite.

"Bullshit, Brad, I know how your kind thinks," Hitt-Man replied while tapping his temple.

"Y'all knock that shit off, here Mr. Lei comes," Caleb said to them without taking his eyes off the Chinaman, who'd appeared from seemingly out of thin air. Caleb smiled at Wang and outstretched his hand. "Mr. Lei, it's a pleasure to meet chu again."

Wang Lei was a Chinaman with a shiny bald head and no facial hair to speak of. He stood five-foot-seven and had a stocky build. Oval-shaped Cartier glasses decorated his face. He was inked in colorful Chinese artwork from his neck down to his ankles. He wore a platinum choker necklace with his "W. L." initials hanging sideways from it. Besides the jewelry, he was wearing an open, short black sportscoat that showcased his bare tattooed chest and slacks.

"The pleasure's all mine, Caleb." Wang smiled as he shook Caleb's hand with both of his. "And, please, call me

Wang." He placed his hand on his chest. "I'd like to sincere-ly apologize for Tree's transgressions. I'll have to have a serious talk with him."

Caleb's face wrinkled, and he waved him off like it wasn't a big deal. "Aw, don't worry about it."

Wang introduce himself to Hitt-Man and Brad and shook their hands. "Please, follow me." He motioned for them to follow him. He led them toward a table at the back of the restaurant where there were two Chinese niggaz with M-16s standing guard. They were dressed in black caps, black undershirts, bulletproof vests, and combat boots.

Two Chinese women with their hair styled in a bun and bang approached the table Wang had in mind. One was wearing a silk, green hanfu robe with a fire-breathing dragon on the back of it. The other one was wearing a silk, blue hanfu robe with a painted-face Chinaman holding a sword on the back of it. Both of the women were carrying bowls of Chinese food they were placing upon the table among others. Once all the food was on the table, the Chinese women stood by with their hands held at their waists.

"Please, have a seat." Wang motioned with the blunt as he sat down.

Caleb and Brad sat down, but Hitt-Man opted to stand. He wanted the same advantage the Chinese niggaz with the M-16s had standing up.

"Are you all hungry?" Wang asked, then pointed at each food item on the table. "We have chicken chow mein, chashu, wonton soup, egg foo yung, pork fried rice. And to drink, we have Baijiu, it's a favorite in China."

"You've provided a feast," Caleb said, looking over the delicious dishes on the table. "Everything looks tasty. I cannot thank you enough, Wang. But, listen, I'd much rather get down to business. Is it alright if we take a couple of doggy bags on our way out?"

Wang sucked on his blunt and blew smoke up at the ceiling. "Sure. No problem." He looked to the women and said something in their native tongue. They bowed and started removing the dishes from off the table, one by one. Once the table was clear, the Chinese woman in the green hanfu returned to the table with a silver platter. Upon it was a brown packaged kilo with a yellow smiley face sticker on it. Beside it was a Gemstar razor blade and small Arrow Head bottled water.

The Chinese woman sat the platter on the table and stood upright, waiting for her boss's orders. Wang told her in Chinese that she was dismissed. She smiled, bowed, and took her leave.

"Brad, go ahead and do yo' thang, my man," Caleb told him, gesturing towards the kilo.

"Say less," Brad replied, licking his lips and anxiously rubbing his hands together. All eyes were on him as he opened the pouch on his side and took out the items he'd need to shoot the dope. He cooked the heroin in a spoon, let a cotton ball soak it up, and drew the liquid contents into the syringe. Next, he sat the syringe upon the table top and picked up the beige tourniquet. He tied it around his arm and pulled it tight with his teeth. He then smacked the inside of his arm, and a thick vein rose before his eyes. Brad eyeballed the vein in his arm as he picked up the syringe. He pressed the needle of the syringe into his vein and immediately, blood clouded it. The plasma turned the heroin burgundy.

Brad pushed down on the feeder until the syringe was empty. As soon as the dope mingled with his system, he threw his head back and his eyes rolled to the back of his head. His hand fell to his side, leaving the tourniquet around his arm and the syringe hanging out of it.

A big smile stretched across his thin pink lips and showcased his mouthful of rotting teeth. Licking his lips, he stuck his hand under his shirt and felt himself up. His hand traveled down to his crotch and he started groping himself sexually. That Chinese dope had him feeling good—real good! Suddenly, his eyes became as big as golf balls and his mouth flew open.

"What the fuck is going on?" a wrinkle-browed Hitt-Man asked Caleb.

Caleb didn't say a damn thing. His attention was focused on Brad and his reaction to the dope.

Brad fell backwards in his chair and spilled out onto the floor. His eyelids fluttered rapidly, showing whiteness. He started convulsing! His lips twisted in an incongruous manner while his heart pounded harder than usual. He breathed erratically and brought his hand up, fingers taking the shape of claws. He made gurgling noises and foam overflowed out of his mouth, forming a pool on the floor. He continued to convulse for a while, until he abruptly stopped. The foam slowly stopped flowing out of his mouth until it dripped below him.

"Hitt, check 'em out," Caleb told him as he brought his arm over the back of the chair.

Hitt-Man placed two fingers on the pulse of Brad's neck. He looked up at Caleb and shook his head. Brad's ass was dead!

Wang clapped his hands, and the Chinese women in the hanfus appeared. They each grabbed an end of Brad's lifeless body and carried him off somewhere into the backroom. The one in the green hanfu returned with a mop in a yellow bucket of soapy water and a yellow wet-floor sign. She slapped the soaking wet mop onto the floor and went about the task of cleaning up the mess.

"Chinese heroin, huh?" Caleb said, looking at the package of dope.

"Yes, sir, the best heroin there ever was," Wang assured him before sucking on his blunt.

Man, if this shit that potent, I'ma have to cut it to about seventy-five percent. Even then, it will still be that fire, Caleb thought as he massaged his chin and stared out the corner of his eye.

"I'm not gon' bullshit chu, Wang. I'm feeling this product," Caleb told him as he toyed with the Gemstar razor on the platter. "So, I'ma need you to get the big dog onna jack. Tell 'em I want 'em for the cheapest he can give 'em to me for."

"I was given permission to negotiate on behalf of Mr. Happy," Wang told him. "So, we can make a deal right here and right now."

"Good." Caleb nodded and continued to toy with the razor blade.

"How many are you looking to get?" Wang blew smoke out the side of his mouth.

Caleb stared at the table top as he thought on it for a moment. "Twenty."

"I'll tell you what," Wang began, "if you purchase thirty of them, I'll give them to you ten a wop."

The bricks of Chinese heroin went for sixty gees a pop all day in the streets, so Caleb stood to make a hell of a profit from each one, especially after he cut them. The offer was too good to pass up, so he had to take it.

Caleb dropped the razor blade onto the platter and stood up from his seat. He smiled and extended his hand. "You've got yourself a deal," he told Wang.

Wang switched hands with the blunt and rose to his feet, shaking Caleb's hand.

Caleb and Wang agreed to make the exchange three days later.

After Caleb left the restaurant, he arranged a meeting with a local hitta by the name of Hellraiser. He and his crew had been doing hits for him for years. He always used them to get the job done. They were the best at what they did and proved to be reliable.

Caleb needed some Jamaican gangstas hit that controlled the heroin trade in the same territory he had his eyes on. He figured once he had them knocked off, he'd be able to take over their turf and move his product without interference.

***

A couple of Chinese niggaz pulled up across the street from a park. They were sitting directly across the street from a Jeep Grand Cherokee. This was the vehicle they were told the loot for the drugs would be stashed. One of them was to make sure the truck had the money in its hatch before delivering it to the location provided. The next person was to drop the payment off to Handz and take the rental back to the company it was rented from.

"That's it, a tan '99 Jeep Grand Cherokee," the Chinese cat behind the wheel told his comrade. His hands were resting on the steering wheel, and in one of them was a piece of paper with the information on it. "The key is supposed to be on the back tire. Get it and pop the hatch to see if money is there."

"Alright," the other Chinese cat said before jumping out of the car. He waited until an oncoming car passed him and jogged across the street to the Jeep Cherokee. He grabbed the key off the back tire, unlocked the hatch, and looked inside. He found a duffle bag! Once he unzipped the bag and saw the money, he turned to the other Chinese man and gave him a thumbs up. Next, he slammed the hatch, jumped in behind the wheel, and peeled off.

The Chinese dude he came with pulled off behind him, punching numbers on his cellphone. He called the man that was next to Mr. Happy.

"Aye, we got it. Be sure to tell them we're on our way now." He disconnected the call, sat his cellular in the passenger seat, and cranked up the volume on a song he liked.

***

Once the Chinese had gotten their loot, they hit Caleb with the information he needed to get his goods. He immediately sent out Hitt-Man and two of his most trusted goons to secure his purchase.

Hitt-Man circled the Del Amo Mall parking lot with JayDee in the passenger seat. He was a golden-brown-skinned nigga who chose to sport a bald head thanks to his receding hairline. The piece of paper with the information they were given was in his hand. He looked back and forth between it and the parked cars they coasted by.

"Damn, you still don't see this mothafucka?" Hitt-Man asked about the car they were told the work would be inside of. He had a blue-raspberry Tootsie Roll pop in one hand and the steering wheel in the other.

"Nah, maybe it's on the other side of this row," JayDee said.

"I don't know, man. I'm starting to think these chinks fucked us." Hitt-Man's face balled up and he clenched his

22

jaws. The muscles in his jaws pulsated. The thought of someone thinking they could pull some fuck shit on his crew made him want to murder something. He already had it in mind to snatch up that nigga Handz and torture his yellow ass until he told him where he could find Mr. Happy.

"Yo, I think that's it right there!" Hot Boy said excitedly from the backseat. He was leaning toward the window on the left side of him, pointing at a parked silver '97 Cadillac Seville CTS. It was sitting on stock rims and yellow and white tires. Hot Boy was two shades darker than his road dog, JayDee. He sported a clean-shaven face with a thin mustache and a fade.

Hitt-Man and JayDee's heads snapped in the direction Hot Boy was pointing. They seemed disappointed when they laid eyes on the vehicle he'd pointed out.

"Nah, that's the right make and model, but it's the wrong color," JayDee told him. "The one we're looking for is charcoal gray. That one is silver."

"Bruh, you've been pointing out the wrong rides since we got to this bitch. Maybe yo' ass needa consider getting some contacts or corrective lenses or some shit," Hitt-Man said. "Goddamn, nigga, you couldn't pick out the nigga that robbed you inna line up if he was six-seven with a pink afro, wearing a neon-green sweatsuit." He shook his head in disappointment.

While Hitt-Man and Hot Boy went back and forth throwing insults at one another, JayDee continued to keep an eye out for the automobile they were looking for. He craned his head to the right as the whip they were in coasted by another row of parked cars.

"Stop!" JayDee told Hitt-Man.

"What?" Hitt-Man asked.

"I said stop, stop the fucking car!" JayDee told him again. "That's the car. There that bitch go right there." He pointed to the car they were looking for. It was the exact one in the picture they'd been given.

"Ayo, make yo'self useful. Get cho ass out the car and go get the shit," Hitt-Man told Hot Boy.

Hot Boy bounced out the car, talking shit under his breath and tucking his gun at the front of his jeans. He found the key to the Cadillac on top of its back tire on the driver's side. He didn't waste any time popping the trunk and lifting it open. He found two copper-brown leather duffle bags inside the trunk.

"Is the shit there or what, nigga?" Hitt-Man called out to him.

"Damn, nigga, gimme a chance to unzip the bags first," a frowning Hot Boy complained while looking over his shoulder at Hitt-Man's whip. He unzipped the duffle bags and looked inside of them. They were loaded with Saran-wrapped kilos with a yellow smiley face sticker on them. A big smile spread across his face when he feasted his eyes on the merchandise.

"My nigga, fuck is up? Is the shit there or what?" an irritated JayDee asked. He was staring at Hot Boy's back while he was going through the duffle bags.

Hot Boy slammed the trunk closed and turned around to Hitt-Man and JayDee. "It's all here! Let's roll." He ran around to the driver's door and snatched it open. Once he jumped behind the wheel, he fired it up and swung out of the spot in reverse. He then shifted into drive and peeled off. Hitt-Man pulled off right behind him, hitting up Caleb on his cellphone. He reported to him that they had the drop.

Mission accomplished!

Chapter Two
Two nights later

The Rude Bwois were a drug crew that had built quite the reputation for themselves. Their organization had made millions of dollars pushing dope in the Low Bottoms. Caleb did his homework, so he knew the Rastas were making a fortune. He figured if he took them out of the equation, and replaced their soldiers and drugs with his own, he'd be rolling in dirty money.

Caleb had a mental rolodex of killaz he could have enlisted for the job, but he wanted the best of the best. Hellraiser and his pack of blood-thirsty dogs laid claim to this exclusive title. They called themselves "Da Crew" and were considered Hall of Famers in the murder game.

Da Crew had been doing business with Caleb for as long as they could remember, so they were up for any gig he had for them. When their leader, Hellraiser, had gotten the call, all he could see was dollar signs. The bag they were going to get hit with was more than worth it for the job they were going to do. Needless to say, although they'd been contacted for the assignment on such short notice, they still agreed to take it.

Hellraiser stood before the mirror of the dresser massaging his chin and looking over his reflection. At thirty-five years old, he stood six feet, had brown skin, and a body ripped with muscles. He wore his hair in six cornrows, and his five o'clock shadow was neatly trimmed. His name was Treymaine James, but he was renowned throughout his hood and the territories of his enemies as Hellraiser, on the account of his acts of brutality. It was that and the fact that he'd seen the original 1985 classic film of the same name exactly one hundred times since its release and had gotten the iconic Pinhead tattooed on his back.

Hellraiser had the status of a killa. He was about that action. When it was war time, there wasn't anyone you would rather have on your side than him. Though his accuracy with a gun was unmatched, his skill with a razor was impeccable. He'd been playing razor tag since youth authority, leaving those who foolishly crossed him bearing his mark. Often, while he was in the streets, civilians would believe he was sucking on a piece of candy, but it would actually be a Gemstar razor inside his mouth. He could spit that baby in his palm and go across a nigga's jugular with it. And by the time the poor bastard realized he'd been cut, he'd already be gone.

Hellraiser whipped off his towel and finished drying off before he tossed it aside. Fully nude, he went about the task of getting dressed in all-black attire for the night's mission. He got dressed in a pair of black Dickies, a black T-shirt, black Nike Cortez, and a hoodie.

"Come here, you lil' black-ass mothafucka, I'ma beat cho ass!" Hellraiser heard his baby mama, Shaniqua, hollering at someone. Hellraiser quickly bounced up from the bed and grabbed his shotgun. He threw open his bedroom door and hurried into the kitchen.

"Aaaahhh! Aaahhhhh! Aahhhhh!" four-and-a-half-year-old KiMani sobbed and screamed horrifically. He held up his hands and feet as his mama hollered at him and whipped him viciously with a white extension cord, which was wrapped around her fist. The cord whistled back and forth through the air, stinging the poor child like the end of a scorpion's tail. Welts overlapped each other on his arms and legs and slowly bled. "No, no, no, Mommy, I'm sorry! I'm sorry!" KiMani sobbed aloud with tears running out of his eyes and green snot bubbles coming out of his nose.

"Yo, what the fuck are you doing? Have you lost your goddamn mind?" Hellraiser roared and grabbed her wrist before she could attack their son with the extension cord again.

"Lemme go, lemme go, goddamn it!" Shaniqua shouted harshly, spit flying from her lips. Her hair was sprawled wildly over her face and shoulders. Her eyes were glassy and red webbed. There were small ropes of slimy saliva hanging from her bottom lip and chin. The bitch looked like a demon in a woman's body.

"Fuck you beating on our son like he Kunta Kinte for?" a scowling Hellraiser asked. KiMani got up on his feet and ran behind his father, holding onto his leg for dear life. He continued to sob with snot oozing out of his nose and over his lips. Some of the shit ran underneath his chin and onto his tiny chest. His heart was beating hard, and he was trembling.

"He spilt all of that shit on the goddamn floor!" Shaniqua told him, raining spittle on his face. "I told his lil' ass I'd give 'em some juice inna minute, but his hardheaded ass went and tried to pour some anyway! Look at my floor now, after I done mopped it up! Lemme go, Treymaine, I'm not done with that lil' bastard yet!" She shot daggers at KiMani, frightening him. He hid further behind his father and sobbed louder.

Hellraiser looked toward the refrigerator and saw a pitcher of Kool-Aid spilled on the floor. A sippie cup with its lid missing was lying beside it. He assumed KiMani was pouring something to drink and accidentally dropped the pitcher.

"Yo, you beat my son like that over some fucking juice?" He eye fucked her like he wanted to blow a hole in her with his shotgun. "You gotta be off yo' meds! Where they at? You taking them shits right now!"

"I flushed them down the toilet!" Shaniqua spat. "I'm not taking that shit no more, I don't need it!"

"You obviously do, the way you hurt my lil' man!"

Shaniqua shut up and looked up to the ceiling. The look in her eyes told him she was frustrated and was ready to attack him.

"On some for real shit, Treymaine, if you don't lemme go, I'ma bomb on yo' ass! My right hand to God, bro. You must think I'm that other bitch you be laying up with," Shaniqua said, tapping her foot impatiently and balling her fist tight. She tightened her jaw and a vein pulsated at the center of her forehead.

"I'm not letting you go unt—" Hellraiser was cut short by Shaniqua unexpectedly punching him in his left eye. He stumbled backwards, discombobulated and seeing a blinding white light. She tried to grab the shotgun from him and a panic alarm went off in his head. He knew she was deadly when she was off her medication and could possibly blow him and his son away, so he held fast to it. Gripping the shotgun with both hands, she kicked him in his balls as hard as she could. "Ooof!" Hellraiser's eyes nearly leaped out of his head and he gasped, bent over, grabbing his precious jewels with one hand. He maintained his hold on the shotgun with one hand until she kicked him in the temple. Hellraiser hurled toward the side quickly. The kitchen floor came up fast, smashing into him. He lay on his side holding himself, squaring his jaws, with a forehead covered in veins. The pain was intense, and it felt like his testicles were lodged in his stomach. "You—you fucking bi—bitch."

Shaniqua took the shotgun by both hands and racked it. She turned around to KiMani. The boy had seen in many movies what guns did to people, and he instantly became terrified. He threw up his hands and slowly walked backward. Fresh tears consumed his eyes and slid down his cheeks over the drying ones. The snot on his lips turned lime green and had begun to crust.

"No, no, no, no, please, Mommy! I'm sorry," KiMani said frantically. "I—I won't do it no—no more!"

"You say that every time you fuck up, KiMani, every time!" Shaniqua said, looking crazy as fuck, taking calculated steps in his direction. "Well, I'ma make sure yo' lil' bad ass don't do it no more." She glanced down between his legs and saw urine dripping. A sick part of her got some pleasure seeing her son so terrified of her.

The truth was, she had been abusing the boy to get back at his father for choosing his main chick over her. She couldn't find it in herself to kill his father because she was obsessed with him and didn't want to be alive without him. So, she figured the best way for her to get back at him was through their son, who looked exactly like him.

"Goodbye, lil' man, Momma loves you," Shaniqua told him, applying pressure to the trigger.

"Aahhhhh!" Hellraiser hollered as he tackled Shaniqua and lifted the shotgun up. As soon as he did, it discharged at the ceiling and debris rained down. His balls were aching something crazy, so he was still pretty weak, but it was the love he had for his son that drove him on. He and Shaniqua grunted and groaned as they fought for control over the shotgun. KiMani ran into the corner of the living room and slid down to the floor. He whimpered as he held his knees to his chest. His innocent eyes watched as his parents fought against each other.

"Let it go, let it go now, goddamn it!" Shaniqua gritted her teeth and tried her best to yank the shotgun from him. She tried to kick him in his balls again, but he shielded himself with his knee.

"You're fucking crazy, Shaniqua, you need some fucking help!" Hellraiser told her through gritted teeth.

"You don't give a fuck about me! And whatever love you do have, it's for that bitch and him!" Shaniqua said. She was talking about his main woman, Lachaun, and their son, KiMani. Her adrenaline was pumping like crazy, so she was slowly winning the battle of control over the shotgun. Hellraiser realized he had to act fast. His and his son's lives were in danger.

"Grrrrrr—" a growling Hellraiser slammed his forehead into Shaniqua's, and she stumbled back. She had a stunned look on her face, and a red lump began to form on her forehead. She felt a migraine coming on, and she was seeing double. Before she could regain her composure, Hellraiser ran up and kicked her in the chest as hard as he could. She flew backward and knocked the plaster out of the wall, causing debris to fall to the floor. Right after, he rushed in, slamming the barrel of the shotgun into her stomach and wacking her across the head with its stock. She hit the floor hard, groaning, with her eyes rolled to the back of her head.

Hellraiser stood, looking down at her and holding his aching nut sack. Hearing footsteps coming up fast behind him, he turned around in time to see KiMani running to him. He scooped his little man up and hugged him to his body. He kissed all over the side of his face and told him how much he loved him.

"Daddy, what's wrong? What's wrong with Mommy?" KiMani asked as he held his father's neck.

"Mommy's sick, son. Mommy's really, really sick," he replied, looking down at Shaniqua, who was now knocked out cold.

"We gotta go to the doctor to get her some medicine so she can feel better," KiMani said.

"We will, son. We will," Hellraiser told him. Right then, his cellular rang, and he looked at its screen. It was Lachaun. He answered it. "Alright, I'll be down there inna minute, but, yo, I'ma have to bring the prince with me. I'll explain everything later. Peace." He disconnected the call and put his jack up. "Hey, how 'bout we go to Granny's house, huh? You wanna spend the night over Granny's house?"

"Granny's house, yaye!" KiMani cheered excitedly and threw his arms in the air. His face was a mess, but he still managed to be in high spirits. He loved his grandma Ruby as much as he loved his parents—maybe even more.

"Okay, we've gotta get chu cleaned up first."

"Okay," KiMani replied. He looked down at Shaniqua, who was still out cold. "What Mommy doing? Why she lying onna floor?"

"It's okay, baby boy, Mommy's just taking a nap," he assured him, kissing his cheek. "Why don't chu go get the blanket off the bed so I can tuck her in."

"A'wight," KiMani said. He ran toward his parents' bedroom as soon as his father sat him down.

This bitch is a reallll piece of work, Hellraiser thought as he propped his shotgun up against the wall. He scooped Shaniqua up in his arms and laid her down on the couch. KiMani ran back into the living room, dragging the blanket along. His father thanked him with a kiss and spread the blanket over his mother. They were about to leave out of the living room when KiMani suddenly ran over to Shaniqua and kissed her on the cheek.

31

"I love you, Mommy," KiMani told her. He then grabbed his father's hand and led him toward the bathroom. "Come on, Daddy, so you can wash me up."

Hellraiser grinned as his little man pulled him along. The grin evaporated from his face once he saw the bruising on his child's back. His forehead wrinkled, and he kneeled down to his son.

"What's wrong, Daddy?" KiMani asked to why his father was turning him around.

"I see you got some boo-boos, I just wanna check 'em out," Hellraiser told him as he focused his attention on his back. There were old burns on the back of his neck that looked like they came from a cigarette. There were also old burns on his back and between his thighs from a curling iron. Hellraiser had been so occupied with running the streets getting money and lying up with Lachaun, that he neglected to make sure his son was okay. The revelation hurt him to the core of his soul. He hated himself for allowing what had happened to his son to occur right under his nose. He didn't know how long his baby boy had been subjected to his mother's torture, but he gathered it had been a while. Shaniqua had hidden it well from him. He took care of all the bills, but she took care of the household and their son. Most times he saw his son was on his way to bed or waking up.

Hellraiser broke down sobbing and sniffling. A concerned KiMani turned around to him, wondering what was wrong with him. His small hands cupped his face and lifted it up. He could see himself in his father's pupils.

"I'm sorry, son. I'm so, so sorry for your boo-boos," Hellraiser told him. "I shoulda been there, man. I shoulda been there to protect you, prince."

"It's okay, Daddy. Don't cry," KiMani told him, wiping the tears from his father's face. He then kissed him on his forehead and both of his cheeks like Hellraiser always did him when he hurt himself. "I'm going to be a'wight. Everything is gonna be okay. A'wight?" Hellraiser shut his eyes and tears jetted down his cheeks. He nodded in agreeance, and KiMani hugged him. "I love you, Daddy."

"I love you too, lil' man. You're my heart, my soul, my life…the air that I breathe," he swore, kissing him on his cheek and hugging him to his body. "Come on, baby boy, let's get chu cleaned up."

Hellraiser gathered underwear and clothes for KiMani. He then got a washcloth and a towel for him to dry off with. The entire time he was washing his son up, the boy could tell something was disturbing him, but he assured him he was okay.

"I'll be right back, baby boy." Hellraiser kissed his son on his forehead while he played with his toys in the tub.

A scowling Hellraiser headed for the bathroom door but stopped when his son called for him. He put on a happier expression and turned around to his boy.

"Yes, son."

"Where are you going?"

"To check on Mommy."

"Oh, okay."

Once Hellraiser had disappeared from out of the bathroom, he darted inside of the bedroom where he'd stashed the shotgun before he began bathing his son. He grabbed the shotgun from underneath the mattress and ran inside of the living room. Fresh tears warmed his cheeks, and his nostrils flared. He yanked the blanket back from a sleeping Shaniqua's body and pressed the barrel of the shotgun into her cheek.

"You fucking bitch, I'ma blow yo' fucking head off for what chu did to our boy," Hellraiser said through gritted

33

teeth. His eyebrows slanted and his nose wrinkled. He gripped his shotgun so tight, his knuckles cracked and it shook slightly. His eyes turned pink and tears constantly flowed down his face. "How could you? How could you hurt someone that loves you unconditionally? Someone so innocent? Someone who doesn't want anything from you but for you to love 'em? Huh?"

"Daddy? Daddyyyyy?" he heard KiMani calling for him.

Hellraiser's cellphone rang and vibrated with a text message then. He was convinced this was a sign from God that he wasn't supposed to body Shaniqua's ass. That, and the fact that she could still get her shit together and salvage her relationship with their son.

Hellraiser took a deep breath and wiped the wetness from his eyes. He lowered his shotgun and pulled out his cellular. It was Lachaun.

Lachaun: *Babe, what's up?*

Hellraiser: *I'm finna get lil' man out the tub and dressed. I'll be out inna sec.*

Lachaun: *K.*

"Daddyyyy?"

Hellraiser smiled hearing his son's sweet voice. The sound of it warmed his heart. He put his jack back up and turned toward the bathroom.

"Yes, son?" Hellraiser called out to his prince.

"I'm wrinkly now. I think it's time I get out!" KiMani replied.

"Okay, son, I'll be right there," he told him with a smile. He then turned to Shaniqua, who was softly snoring. "You gon' get cho mind right and do right by our son. 'Cause if not, I swear I'ma hunt cho ass down and putta bullet in yo' fucking head."

Hellraiser retreated to the bedroom and stashed the shotgun underneath the mattress. He then headed back inside of the bathroom where he tickled his son. They both laughed and splashed water at each other.

***

"Say, bruh, we can't take nephew with us on no mission," Mack said when Hellraiser passed him KiMani and got into the van. Mack was a dark caramel-complexioned dude from the island of Cuba. He wore his hair in a fade and had deep waves. His fashion-model good looks and bad-boy demeanor made him a favorite among the ladies. Under the thumb of a veteran in the game that had taken a liking to him, Mack learned all he needed to know about busting a bitch and putting her under his instructions. A short time later, he had a stable of thirteen bitchez. Although dealing with so many whores with wants, needs, and complaints was stressful, the money was fast and plentiful.

Mack had mastered The Art of Macking, so the game had gotten boring for him. That's why he added hit-man to his resume. He loved the euphoric feeling he got from taking a nigga's life more so than he loved the one he got from breaking a ho for a grip.

"No shit, Sherlock," Hellraiser said. "I'ma drop 'em off at my mom's crib then we're gon' bust this move."

"Hey, baby boy, how're you?" a smiling Lachaun asked KiMani. She then fired the van up and pulled out into traffic. At twenty-five years old, she was easily the youngest of Da Crew by ten years. Thanks to her skills in martial arts and her exceptional aim with a firearm, she was also one of its most deadly. One minute, the chocolate beauty would be seducing a mark with her enchanting eyes and breathtaking smile, and the next, she'd be blowing his brains out.

"Heyyy, Chaun," KiMani said excitedly. He smiled and hugged her around the neck, kissing her on the cheek. She smiled and kissed him back. "Hey, Uncle Mack, Uncle Julian, and Uncle Saint," he greeted his father's best friends and stuck out his fist for dap. All of his uncles dapped him up and greeted him.

"Wanna come back here with us, nephew?" a jovial Julian asked. He had the typical good kid that fell in with the wrong crowd story. Although he came up in one of the most dangerous neighborhoods in Southern Cali, he was fortunate enough to have both parents in the household. They did everything a happy and loving family did together. During the weekends and summers off from school, Julian would work at Old Man Griffith's bar, Bottoms Up. He was actually too young to have a gig at the bar, but his age went unnoticed due to his charming personality. His job was to sweep and mop the floor, serve drinks, and take inventory.

The gig was fulfilling for Julian during his time off from school, but a future incident would change his career path forever. One night, Julian was left to close up shop since Old Man Griffith's daughter was coming home from college and he had to pick her up from LAX airport. Julian had just pulled the shutter down when he saw a masked Hellraiser running up the street with a gun and a bloody brown paper bag. A police car was on his ass and he was looking around for somewhere to hide. Not wanting another black man to fall victim to the law, Julian hid him inside of the bar until the police cleared the scene.

Thankful that he'd saved him from doing a bid, Hellraiser gave him a handful of dead faces from his bag. The money had bloody fingerprints on it, so Julian knew it was dirty. He didn't care, though. As far as he was concerned, money was money! A couple of weeks later, Hellraiser and Mack ran into Julian while they were playing basketball at the YMCA on 28th Street. They started chopping it up as they shot the ball around. Hellraiser asked Julian if he was interested in making some money robbing a crack house. He was with it. Once Julian got his first taste of dirty money, he never looked back. He was addicted!

KiMani looked to his father for approval.

"You wanna go back there witcho uncles, son? You can go—gone," Hellraiser told him. KiMani outstretched his arms for one of his uncles to get him. Mack grabbed him and sat him in between himself and Julian. Mack was smoking a blunt while Julian had a fifth of Hennessy in a wrinkled brown paper bag. They'd been passing the weed and alcohol among each other. They preferred to be shit faced before every kill strike they launched.

"Yo, what's up with lil' man? Why couldn't he have stayed with Shaniqua?" Lachaun asked in a hushed tone as she looked between him and the windshield.

"I caught her ass in the kitchen beating my lil' nigga ass with an extension cord." Hellraiser replied, glassy eyed. "She beat 'em so bad that the welts that formed over his body started to blister and bleed! When I saw how she was doing him, it was like—it was like she was a completely different person. If I didn't know any better, I'd say she was possessed by an evil spirit then. But, I know better."

"She stopped taking her meds?" Lachaun inquired. She knew about Shaniqua and her mental health issues. There wasn't any secret that she suffered from bipolarism and schizophrenia.

"Yeah. She's been off them shits for a while," Hellraiser told her. "I can't have her around our son anymore. There's no telling how long she's been abusing him. One day, she could possibly kill 'em. Lord knows if that was to happen, a nigga would never be able to forgive himself."

Lachaun grasped Hellraiser's hand lovingly. "What chu say to her before you left?"

"Nothing. I knocked her ass out cold," Hellraiser told her like it was no big deal that he'd TKO'd his baby mama.

Lachaun's eyes bulged with shock and her mouth hung opened when he said this. "For real?"

Hellraiser nodded and said, "Yep. The bitch tried to shoot me. So, it was either that or—"

"Yeah, you can't do that," Lachaun replied as she nodded understandingly.

"I'ma see if my moms minds if I crash at her crib while I see about getting full custody of KiMani."

"Babe, you and KiMani don't have to hole up at cho mother's house. You know you can stay with me."

"The thought came to mind, but I don't wanna be a burden to you."

"Boy, please, I'd love to have y'all crashing with me."

"You sure?"

"Hell yes, I'm sure," Lachaun assured him. "What woman in her right mind gon' turn down some in-house dick?" She licked her lips seductively and grasped his bulge, causing him to grunt. He looked over at her and grinned.

KiMani went into a coughing fit. He was pink eyed and tears threatened to slide down his face. Hellraiser looked over his shoulder into the backseat at him. Mack and Saint were laughing their asses off while a smiling Julian was patting KiMani's back.

"Lil' nigga can't handle the weed. Like father, like son," Mack said with the blunt pinched between his finger and thumb. "Ain't that right, Trey?" Hellraiser gave him a "whatever, mothafucka" look and held up his middle finger.

"I know y'all not giving that lil' boy no weed?" Lachaun asked angrily.

"Absolutely not! What the fuck do you take us for?" Julian said like he was offended she asked. He then ruffled KiMani's head and smiled. "We gave this lil' nigga some chronic." He busted up laughing along with Mack and Lil' Saint.

"You ain't gon' stop that?" Lachaun asked Hellraiser, who was staring at his son grinning. He watched as Julian gave him a swallow of the Hennessy, which made his eyes bulge. He then stuck out his tongue like it was hot and started fanning it. This seemed to make Mack and them laugh.

"Nah, he's hadda rough night. Let 'em enjoy his time with his uncles," Hellraiser told her, keeping his eyes on KiMani and his uncles.

"I bet cho lil' ass don't won't no more, huh?" Julian said with his arm around KiMani's shoulders.

KiMani wiped his wet mouth and looked at the Hennessy bottle in Julian's hand. He nodded yes and stuck his hands out to receive it.

"Hahahahahaha!" Julian threw his head back, laughing heartily.

"Hahahahahaha!" Lil' Saint doubled over laughing, holding his stomach.

"Hahahahahaha!" Mack laughed aloud, stomping his foot and smacking the seat. He then wiped the tears of laughter from his eyes.

Still staring at KiMani, who was about to take another sip of the Hennessy, Hellraiser laughed. Lachaun looked up at the rearview mirror to see KiMani having the same reaction he had from his first swallow of the brown liquor. When Julian tried to give him some more, he turned his head and shoved the bottle away.

Lachaun laughed and shook her head.

Chapter Three

By the time Lachaun made it to Hellraiser's mother's house, KiMani was slumped between Mack and Julian. He was drooling at the corner of his mouth and snoring softly.

"Look at 'em back there knocked out. He's so cute," Lachaun declared, looking into the backseat at KiMani.

"Yeah, that's my lil' man right there. I love 'em to death," a smiling Hellraiser said, staring at his son as well. The smile left his face when he saw Lachaun's expression change into a serious one. "What's up, babe?"

"Look at 'em, babe. He's so young and innocent. Lil' man hasn't experienced enough of life to make his heart turn cold," Lachaun assessed. "The way that girl beat him like he was an unruly slave, that baby didn't deserve that—" Her voice cracked emotionally and a tear descended down her left cheek. She wiped it away and cleared her throat. "That baby didn't deserve that, what she did to him." Her eyebrows slanted and her nose scrunched up. She balled her fists, and the veins in them became pronounced. "I swear to God, babe, the next time I see that bitch, I'ma put paws on her ass. See if she likes it when someone's beating on her."

Hellraiser couldn't say anything to what Lachaun had just said. He was as hot as she was behind what Shaniqua had done to their son, and he wanted to splatter her nut ass. He had to remind himself that she wasn't right in the head and she was still his son's mother. He couldn't live with himself knowing he'd taken his boy's mother away from him. Those were the two factors that saved Shaniqua from being murdered and planted inside some hole in the desert somewhere.

"We're looking at the future here, Blood," a grinning Mack swore while looking at KiMani, who was still asleep, drooling.

"When nephew is old enough to start claiming the hood, the opps gon' catch hell," Julian made his observation. He thought about the chaos the boy's father wreaked on the city when they were coming up.

A serious look came over Hellraiser's face while looking at KiMani. He imagined him running the same streets as he had and experiencing the hardships his lifestyle brought him. His mind was assaulted by visuals of the arrests, court appearances, prison riots, fights, shootings, murders, mothers grieving, and funerals he'd witnessed throughout his time as a gangsta. As cliché as it may seem, he'd seen it all and he'd done it all. In fact, he still had nightmares from his chaotic past.

No one should ever strive to be in this lifestyle. Shit was counterproductive, and the only outcome was death or incarceration. *Still, it's the life we know—it's the life we chose, so we accept it. Nah, I want better than that for KiMani. He deserves better than that. And I'll do everything within my power to see to it that he doesn't have to go through the shit I've gone through,* Hellraiser thought as he opened the door of the van and took KiMani from Mack's hands. He kissed his boy on his cheek and hoisted him up on his shoulder.

Hellraiser headed toward his mother's house, but Lachaun calling for him stopped him. He turned around to find her approaching with a smile on her face. She rubbed KiMani's head and kissed him on his cheek.

"Good night, lil' man, sweet dreams, I love you," Lachaun told him and walked back to the van.

Hellraiser smiled at Lachaun as she walked away. There was no doubt in his mind that she was the woman for him, which made what he was about to do tonight easy. He went up the steps and rapped on the door. His mother pulled back the curtain and peeked outside. She smiled when she saw Hellraiser, and he smiled back. She disappeared from the window and a second later, the locks of the front door came undone. A five-foot-two woman opened the door and stepped out onto the porch. Her hair was curled up with pink rollers, and she was dressed in a flower-printed house coat. She was a fifty-five-year-old woman who was still fine for her age. But it was obvious she was even finer in her youth.

"Hey, gorgeous," Hellraiser greeted his mother with a smile.

"Hey, my baby boy," his mother, Ruby, greeted him as he kissed her on the cheek. "Is that my grandson?" she asked, holding up her arms to receive him.

"Yeah, this is him. He's knocked out, too," Hellraiser said as he passed his son to her. He watched as she kissed him and laid him against her shoulder.

"Where you off to, son?" Ruby asked.

"Just to a function with my friends," he lied smoothly.

Lachaun honked the horn to steal Ruby's attention. When she looked in her direction, she hung halfway out of the window waving at her.

"Hey, Mrs. Ruby," Lachaun called out to her.

"Hey, Lachaun." Ruby smiled and waved back at her. "How're you doing?"

"I'm doing okay. How're you?"

"I'm good."

Mack, Lil' Saint, and Julian exchanged pleasantries with Ruby as well. They'd all known her since they were kids, and she treated them all like she'd pushed them out of her womb. It was safe to say they loved her like a mother and treated her like she was theirs.

After conversing with the fellas, Ruby turned to her son and took in his attire. She made note of his all-black clothing. He was dressed in all black and so was Lachaun. She was pretty sure the rest of the fellas were dressed the same as well. She knew that usually when niggaz dressed up in all black, they were going out to do something unlawfully. With her knowing her son's get down, she believed he and his crew were most likely headed to kill someone this night.

Ruby wasn't anyone's fool. She'd been a gangsta's wife for as long as she could remember. As much as she loved Hellraiser's father, she wished she hadn't chosen a man who was entangled with the streets. She reasoned that if she hadn't, then her son wouldn't have chosen to walk the same path as his father before him. She acknowledged it was likely he'd end up dead or with a lifetime behind bars like his old man. That thought alone saddened her, but she couldn't do anything to change her child's circumstances. All she could do was hope and pray that he made it back home safe.

"Function, huh?" Ruby said.

"Yeah, Ma, a function," Hellraiser replied as he scratched behind his ear. His mother knew that whenever he did that, he was lying. It was something he'd done since he was old enough to pee straight.

"Son," Ruby started off, rubbing the side of Hellraiser's face, "I want chu, once and for all, to leave these streets alone and tend to your son. Forgive me for saying this, but if you hadn't been so wrapped up in them, then you'd have noticed that Shaniqua was abusing this child." Hellraiser nodded. There wasn't shit he could say. His mother was absolutely right. "Shaniqua needs help, Treymaine. I'm talking serious, serious help, so she'll definitely be out of the picture for a while—if not forever. 'Cause Lord knows I wouldn't want her alone with KiMani again—not after this ordeal."

"I know, Momma, and I'm done with Shaniqua," Hellraiser said with confidence dripping from his vocals. "It's all about me and Lachaun now. And I've—"

"Treymaine," Ruby interrupted him. "I know you love Lachaun with all your heart. She was a kind, sweet, selfless, and loving young woman."

"Was?" Hellraiser frowned. His mother was speaking in past tense, like his lady had changed.

Ruby adjusted KiMani in her arms. She looked at the ground to try to find the right words to say without offending her son or hurting his feelings.

"I've heard stories about things you've done in the streets. Things I believed only a monster was capable of doing," a glassy-eyed Ruby admitted. "With me having that knowledge, I could only imagine what Lachaun has done to be able to lay claim as your woman. Lord, forgive me, but I've done some unsavory things out of love for your father. Sorry to say, but yo' momma isn't innocent. My hands are stained with blood, too. Luckily, I smartened up and washed my hands of your father, or I'd be behind them walls with 'em," she claimed as tears slowly oozed out of her eyes and down her cheeks. Hellraiser gently swept the tears away with his thumbs. He hated to see his mother brought to tears on account of his actions. The sight was enough to have tears dancing in his eyes. He wouldn't allow them to stain his cheeks. At least not standing there before his mother, he wouldn't. He'd vowed to his old man that he'd always be the protector, provider, and strength that his mother needed when he'd gotten locked up.

"You're right, Momma," Hellraiser hated to admit. "But I swear on the lives of all of those that I love, I'm finna be done. I'm already sitting on a nice lil' stash that I'ma use for investments and opening profitable businesses. I'ma go legit. Wife up Lachaun, and live happily ever after some place far, far away from the ghetto," he said, holding on to his mother's hand and caressing it with his thumb. "I'ma take you with us too, Momma. I want chu to come with us. The kids gon' need their grandmother."

Ruby's eyes widened with surprise as Lachaun honked the horn. Hellraiser turned around, holding up a finger signaling to her to give him a minute.

"Kids? As in more than one?"

"Yeah."

"So, Lachaun is pregnant?"

"Not yet, Momma, but chu know yo' baby boy plans for the future." Hellraiser cracked a smile, and his mother hit him playfully on his shoulder. "Nah, but seriously, Ma, everything is gonna be fine. I promise." He took her hand into both of his and kissed it. He kissed her sweetly on the forehead and then he kissed KiMani. "I love you, Ma," he said, jogging back to the van.

"I love you too, baby boy." Ruby waved goodbye to her son as the van pulled out of the driveway. Lachaun waved goodbye to her, too, and she waved back at her.

Once the van disappeared down the street, Ruby headed back inside of the house and closed the door behind her.

After Ruby laid KiMani down in bed, she was going to say a prayer for her son and his crew. She knew they were going to snatch the lives of some other women's sons, fathers, nephews, and possibly daughters. Still, that wasn't going to stop her from asking God to allow them to accomplish their deathly mission and make it back to their loved ones in one piece. Although Ruby fully acknowledged that her asking The Almighty for something so selfish was wrong, she reasoned she'd rather it was someone else's son than hers.

***

Da Crew switched up vans and headed to their destination. When Lachaun pulled up to the location, they began getting ready for their assignment. Lil' Saint unzipped the long black duffle bag and started handing out ski masks and gloves. Next, he passed out firearms and extra ammunition. Everyone made sure their weapons were locked and loaded. They then pulled the ski masks down over their faces.

"I take it that's them on the basketball court?" Lachaun said. Her attention was focused out of the window where there was a crowd of spectators watching a basketball game.

"Yeah, that's them mothafuckaz out there," Hellraiser confirmed, looking out of the same window as Lachaun. She was the only one with a bare face since she was the getaway driver. "Y'all, listen up." He turned to Mack, Julian, and Lil' Saint. "Y'all go through the entrance of the basketball court while I'll go in through the exit. There are kids and bystanders out there, so watch who y'all shooting. I've done enough shit I've gotta answer for when I see The Man Upstairs, and the last thing I need is innocent blood on my hands."

"Fuck we know who to go after?" Mack asked.

"Easy. Y'all wet up any nigga rocking dreads and/or RB tattoos," Hellraiser informed them. "Those the Rastas Caleb wants blown off the map. Got it?" Da Crew nodded. "Good."

Lachaun suddenly pulled Hellraiser closer and kissed him passionately.

"I love you, babe. Make sure you come back to me," Lachaun told him as she held onto the Draco in her lap.

"Not even death can keep me from you," Hellraiser assured her before kissing her again. When he pulled away from her, he was smiling, until he noticed the mini AK47 in her gloved hand. The jovial expression disappeared from his lips as he realized his mother was more right than he let on. Although Lachaun had grown up in the hood like he had, they weren't of the same upbringing. Her parents made sure she stayed clear of the streets and attended a private school far from their community—somewhere in the valley. She had to wake up at three o'clock every morning to get dressed and be at the pickup point by five for the two-hour ride.

Lachaun maintained a 4.0. She was on the honor roll and soared academically. Her parents were overprotective, so outside of school and after-school programs, she was inside of the house. She had plans to attend college to become a registered nurse, but that was derailed when she met Hellraiser. He was tall, handsome, buff, tatted up, and had that gangsta swag. On top of that, he was a hood celebrity that all the hood rats were trying to get with. So, it was to Lachaun's surprise when he hollered at her.

Hellraiser and Lachaun hung out a few times and winded up smashing. Afterward, they were kicking it every day for the next four months. Lachaun's parents, especially her dad, being an ex-street nigga himself, wasn't feeling the idea of his baby girl dating a thug. He'd forbidden her from seeing Hellraiser, but she wouldn't listen. Her father trying to wedge a gap between her and her man only pushed her into his arms.

Lachaun got so caught up in Hellraiser that she put college on the back burner so she could spend all of her time with him. It wasn't long before she was running the streets with him and hitting licks right beside him. Hellraiser had his hand in every trade in the streets one could possibly imagine: jacking, hustling, scamming, and his bread and butter, whacking niggaz! Being his woman, naturally, Lachaun was involved in everything that he was in. Little mama wasn't a street chick, but she damn sure became one under her man's rule.

The fast life would eventually catch up with Lachaun, and she found herself locked up fighting a murder charge. Things didn't look good for her, but Hellraiser was holding her down. He made sure she had money for commissary and would visit her regularly. Lachaun didn't know how long she'd be incarcerated fighting her charge, so she gave him a pass. He could sex whomever he wanted as long as he strapped up and didn't catch feelings for them. Hellraiser fought his natural cravings for sex for a while, but eventually, he gave in. That's where Shaniqua came in.

Shaniqua was young, fine, hood as fuck, and had that ghetto sex appeal he loved so much. She was loving and caring also, but she had a smart-ass mouth. She was okay once he checked her ass, though. Shorty would get as wet as a faucet when he did that shit, and they'd have the most incredible sex—protected, of course. Unfortunately, on one occasion, the condom broke and Shaniqua winded up getting pregnant. She was going to get rid of it, but Hellraiser wasn't having it. Surprisingly, Lachaun wasn't either. Not only did she not believe in abortions, she didn't want to have an innocent child's death on her conscience.

When Lachaun's mother was killed by a drunk driver on a rainy night, her father lost it and ended up in an asylum. Since she was locked up, there wasn't any way that she could go to her mother's funeral or visit her father. The death of her mother, her father being in a mental hospital, and the possibility of a long prison sentence looming over her head had Lachaun at her wit's end. Feeling depressed and lonely, Lachaun turned to the only person she felt was in her corner—Hellraiser. He was her lover and best friend all in one.

Hellraiser comforted her as best as he could. She felt a little better, but he knew what would really lighten the load on her shoulders—her freedom! With that in mind, he caught up with the witness in her case and sent her on a permanent vacation. A couple of weeks later, Lachaun was a free woman. Shaniqua wasn't ready to let Hellraiser go, though. She threatened to abort the baby traditionally or by her own means.

With that in mind, Hellraiser convinced Shaniqua he was leaving Lachaun so they could become a family. She wholeheartedly believed him, until she became aware of his house hopping. Still, she didn't leave him. She felt like she wasn't just going to let Lachaun have him. That's when she started victimizing KiMani!

"Alright, crew, let's get this money," Hellraiser told the hittaz as he hopped out of the van. Hunched down and cradling their guns, they invaded the foreign territory like they were military trained.

Chapter Four

Jagha was a mahogany-complexioned nigga with a slender body and locs that hung down his back. He had soft brown eyes, a relatively big nose, and an impeccably trimmed goatee. His face was a mask of concentration as he bounced the Spalding basketball. He had twenty gees on the line. The dough was nothing to him, though. He spent that a year on underwear and socks. He was more focused on entertaining the audience that had gathered around to see him compete. Standing to the left of him was his girl, Amoya. Standing to his right was the infamous Jamaican Jimmy, his nephew, Fitzroy, who he had the bet with, and his Rude Bwoi drug clique. They were made up of all Jamaicans that either came over to the United States from the motherland or were born on American soil. They were all with the shits and had a couple of bodies under their belts. They sported long dread locs, short dread locs, nappy high-top fades, baldheads, and RB ink somewhere on their bodies. The RB tattoo stood for "Rude Bwois."

Jagha took a breath, lifted the Spalding, and let it fly. The basketball bounced off one side of the rim to the other and fell into the netless basket. The audience went wild, and Fitzroy dropped his head. One of Jamaican Jimmy's bodyguards stepped forth with the forty gees in his fedora. Jagha grabbed the loot out the hat and kissed it. He handed the money to Amoya, who unzipped the black leather pouch attached to her hip and stashed it.

"Ya win some, ya lose some. It's alla part of dee game. Maybe next time ya come out on top." Jagha extended his hand to Fitzroy.

Fitzroy looked at Jagha's hand as if he'd just scratched his balls with it. He looked into his eyes and said, "Fuck outta here with that good sportsman shit, my nigga. The game ain't over."

Fitzroy was one of the only Rude Bwois present that didn't speak with an accent. This was due to the fact that he was born in America. Although he'd been afforded a better opportunity than his parents, it didn't stop him from running afoul of the law. He ran the streets with a gang of young ruffians doing anything they could to make a dollar and immortalize their names.

Fitzroy was a skinny light-skinned dude with locs that reached the back of his neck. He was wearing a black Phoenix Suns cap with the tags still on it and a matching Charles Barkley Phoenix Suns jersey. An icy gold RB necklace styled like the Bentley emblem dangled from his neck. He had a gold AP Rolex on his left wrist. The face of the timepiece was flooded with diamonds of the same colors that made up the Jamaican flag.

"Well den, let's keep dee show onna road, den. Me gotta 'nough money ta keep shootin' dee ball 'til ya arms fall off, neega. Me tried ta warn ya young ass 'bout fuckin' wit' me. 'Fore da street dreams, me was Michael Jordan back in high school. Ya betta ask somebody, youth." Jagha dribbled the basketball between his legs with expertise. The way he was handling the basketball, everyone could tell he wasn't blowing smoke up Fitzroy's ass. Back in the day, Jagha was nice on the court. In fact, he was predicted to be the next best thing to hit the NBA since Kobe Bryant. His face was on the cover of every sports magazine you could name, and he'd been the talk of the city. It was safe to say that the Rude Bwoi had the world at his feet. Unfortunately, he threw it all away to run the streets. To him, being a superstar basketball player was cool, but being a gangsta was even better.

The hood whispered with talks of Jagha being a god-damn fool for letting the opportunity slip through his fingers, but he didn't care. He was living out his dream. And no matter how dumb of a dream it was, it was his to live. "Me not gon' stop 'til ya leave out dis muddafucka wearin' nothin' but ya socks and britches, bet dat."

"What they hitting for—Pops?" Fitzroy asked, taking a shot at Jagha's age.

"A hunnit gees, neega," Jagha shot back, causing the crowd to say 'Ooooh.'

"I don't have it on me. I'ma have to run up top fa it."

"Nah, fuck all dat." Jagha waved him off. "What's dat? A five-hundred, six-hundred Benz ya pushin'? Dat's wort' prolly fifty, sixty racks. Jewels?" He took inventory of Fitzroy's icy jewels and calculated their worth in his head. "Me say dat's 'bout fifty-five, sixty gees, so ya bettin' or wut?"

"Shiiiiiit, you ain't said nothin' butta word, homeboy," Fitzroy replied.

"Me a holda money and jewelry," Jamaican Jimmy chimed in.

Jamaican Jimmy was a five-foot-eleven nigga with a full, well-kept beard. He had a wide nose, big lips, and freckles covering his face. He sported a receding hairline and six neat cornrows, which he kept underneath a soft, charcoal-gray fedora hat. Gold wire glasses decorated his face and matched perfectly with his gold, plain-face Rolex. He wore a charcoal-gray overcoat over an expensive soft gray suit that fit him to a tee. A thick gold rope hung from his neck with a big pendant of the Jamaican flag. It was flooded with black, yellow, and green diamonds. All of those shits were glisten-ing! At sixty-two years old, Jamaican Jimmy was the grandfather of the Rude Bwois crew. He established the organization when he left the motherland of Jamaica to avoid persecution for a couple of homicides. The Rude Bwois started out as a group to police their own neighborhoods and protect everyone in their community. Unfortunately, like all gangs that were formed on this premise, they ended up becoming the same problem they fought against.

On either side of Jamaican Jimmy was a bodyguard dressed just as debonair as he was. They were a pair of serious-looking cats with a talent for killing that was nearly unmatched. This was the exact reason why Jamaican Jimmy employed them.

"Nah, dat's awright, me gal's got it," Jagha told him. He didn't trust Jamaican Jimmy as far as he could see him. He knew exactly how the old head and his crew of cutthroat Rastas got down, and he wasn't taking any chances.

Amoya stepped forth, blowing a huge pink bubble from her mouth. Once it popped, she sucked it back inside of her mouth and started chewing it again. Her long brown locs were pulled back in a ponytail. She had icy gold "J" earrings in her lobes and an icy gold Cuban-link choker that held onto the nametag "Jagha." Amoya was wearing a waist-length black leather jacket over a see-through, flower-print halter top and skin-tight black leather pants.

Amoya held open a sack and Jagha dumped the rolls of money inside. Fitzroy removed his jewelry and was about to drop it in the bag, but Jagha stopped him. "Hold on, youth." Jagha held up his hand. He snapped his fingers and Amoya pulled out a black device that resembled a handheld metal detector. She took the jewelry from Fitzroy and waved the device like a magic wand over them, and a blue light flashed. Amoya nodded approvingly to Jagha.

"Yo, what the fuck is this?" Fitzroy asked, with furrowed brows.

"Makin' sur' ya shit's not fugazi. Me not sayin' ya would rock sum fake shit, but me can neva be too care'fa, it's jussa lil' precaution."

"Unc, can you believe this nigga?" Fitzroy looked back at Jamaican Jimmy and then back at Jagha, who was watching his bitch inspect the diamonds in his jewelry with a loupe. She was checking the clarity in the stones. Jagha didn't fuck with them cloudy shits. "What chu think? You're the only nigga out here getting to the money? You tryna make a nigga look bad in front of mothafuckaz or something, huh?" he asked with growing animosity, clenching his jaws and balling his fists at his sides.

"We're good," Amoya told Jagha before dropping the jewelry into the bag.

Jagha took the bag and handed it to Amoya. "Me not tryna make ya look bad, youth, dis is business, and me serious 'bout mine. Me can't have anyone runnin' 'round talkin' 'bout dey got won ova on old Jagha, ya feel me, neega, huh?" He smiled and winked at Fitzroy. "Dun't wet it though, Big Time. Ya jewels checked out, like me thought dey would." He looked to Amoya. "We good, beloved?"

"Oh, we're awesome," Amoya said, switching hands with the sack of goods.

"Make sure no won runs off wit' dat bag."

"Anybody tries runnin' off wit' dis bag gon' die froma heat stroke." Amoya tapped the gun on her waistline, drawing everyone's attention to it. If anyone tried to steal that bag from her iron grip, they'd wind up a casualty of a botched robbery.

Jagha snapped his fingers, recalling something. "Oh, almost fa'got. Keys, please." Fitzroy tossed his car keys to Amoya and dropped them into the sack. Jagha smiled and threw the youngsta the ball. "It's on you, Big Time."

Fitzroy turned and faced the basket while bouncing the ball. He stole a glance at Jagha. He had his arms folded across his chest and wore a smirk on his big lips. Fitzroy looked around at all the faces of the people in attendance, and all eyes were on him. It was so quiet you could hear a mosquito pass gas. Fitzroy's heart raged in his chest. The pressure he felt was immense. He wished he hadn't opened his big mouth to Jagha.

***

The Rasta was just passing through the hood like he always did, chopping it up with the people and spreading dollars around to the little ghetto children, when Fitzroy came slithering off the court with his man guzzling a Gatorade and bragging to him about having the illest jumpshot in the city. Jagha asked him to prove it, and he got fly at the mouth.

"*Fucka friendly game! Me and my man just finished running up and down the court underneath this hot-ass sun! I'll tell you what, though, me and you can get a lil' wager going. Best three out of five shots—twenty gees.*"

"*Ya sur' ya tryna take it dere, youth?*" *Jagha asked, smiling devilishly. He was with the shits, so he didn't mind the drama.* "*Me not sur' if ya know, but—*"

"*Yeah, yeah, yeah, I know about your lil' hoop dreams, nigga. I ain't up for going down memory lane witcho old ass. Just put your money where your mouth is.*" *He held up a big ass bankroll secured by a rubber band.*

Amoya went to move on Fitzroy for his blatant disrespect, but Jagha waved her off. "*It's alright, beloved,*" *Jagha said, stripping down to his undershirt.* "*Me 'bouta give his lil' assa spankin' him neva fa'get.*"

56

The Last of the OG's

Fitzroy threw Jagha the basketball, smiled, and nodded to the court. "Come on, Gramps."

Jamaican Jimmy was passing through and decided to hop out of his whip to see what the gathering was about. He was surprised to see his nephew shooting it out with Jagha, who was an acquaintance of his. He figured he'd make it an event and called up some of the other Rude Bwois to spectate the game. Soon, the basketball court was full of people watching the competition between Fitzroy and Jagha.

***

Now, here Fitzroy was after letting his mouth write a check that his ass couldn't cash. If there was one thing he hated most in life, it was losing. He couldn't handle not being the one to come out on top. He was too used to besting others and giving the tongue lashing. Heart pounding in his ears, Fitzroy raised the Spalding and released it from his palms. The basketball hit the backboard and fell into the basket. Jagha applauded him and kicked the ball back out to him.

Fitzroy wiped his sweaty forehead with his shirt, bounced the ball a few times, blew hard, and sank the Spalding into the basket. He put the ball up three more times; making the next two but missing the last one. He smiled, figuring he had the win as he tossed the ball to Jagha and stepped behind the backboard. He thought the best Jagha could do was tie the game or fall short a basket, but there was no way he'd make all five shots. Fitzroy rubbed his hands together and smiled like he knew something that no one else knew. Jagha, on the other hand, wasn't paying him any attention. His mind was on making every shot and coming out of the competition victorious.

By the time Jagha had made his fourth basket, the smile had disappeared from Fitzroy's lips. His eyes held a glimmer of hope when Jagha shot the basketball for the fifth time and it circled the rim. That hope was soon demolished when the ball dropped into the basket and sealed the older Rasta's victory. The crowd went wild, cheering and raising Jagha over their heads. He smiled and laughed, enjoying the praise he got for his win. The crowd lowered him to his feet, and Amoya gave him his sack of winnings. After grabbing something out of it, Jagha slung the sack over his shoulder and tossed Amoya Fitzroy's car keys.

"She's yours," Jagha told her.

"You serious?" Amoya asked with a one-sided smile.

"Yep, happy early birfday, we can go put it in ya name first ting in da mornin'."

"Thank ya, daddy." Amoya kissed his cheek.

"Ya welcome."

Boc!

A shot rang out, startling the spectators and making them back up from the shooter. Fitzroy lowered a smoking revolver from the air and approached Jagha, holding his pistol on him. Amoya's hand inched toward the gun on her waistline, and Fitzroy turned his gun on her.

"Make another move and I'ma blow yo' fucking head off, bitch! Matter of fact, slowly pull that shit out and toss it on the ground," he ordered venomously. Once she'd done as he said, he turned his attention to Jagha. "Hand over that bag." He motioned with his free hand.

Jagha gave Fitzroy his sack of winnings. "Neva figured ya fa a sore losa."

"Shiiiiiit, the way I see it, there's only one loser here." Fitzroy smiled, showcasing a mouthful of perfectly white teeth, which he slid his tongue across. He then held open the sack to check its contents.

"Sho' ya wright," Jagha said, glaring at him. His hand eased toward the gun at the small of his back. Fitzroy was peering inside of the bag while he was attempting to make his move. As soon as Jagha pulled his piece, Fitzroy grunted in pain and collapsed to the ground in a heap. A scowling Jamaican Jimmy stood behind him with his staff in his fist. He kicked the young man's gun from out of his reach and spat off to the side. Fitzroy looked up at his uncle, wincing as he rubbed the back of his aching head. He wondered why his uncle had abruptly attacked him.

"Fuck you hit me for, Unc?" Fitzroy asked, looking confused.

"Ya lost fair and square, bwoi. If ya won den da mon woulda letcha collect ya winnins. Now, get up! Get ya ass up, right now!" He roughly pulled his nephew to his feet.

"Step outta da way, Jamaican Jimmy," Amoya said, trying to get a clear shot at Fitzroy. She'd snatched up her blower as soon as Jamaican Jimmy had attacked Fitzroy.

Jamaican Jimmy's head whipped from Amoya to Jagha. He drew the katana from the gold cobra-head staff and stepped between Fitzroy and the guns meant to knock his wig off. As soon as he did, he heard his killaz cocking back the hammers of their bangaz. He glanced over his shoulder and found the Rude Bwois there. They were mad dogging Jagha and Amoya while keeping their guns on them.

"Move outta dee way, Jamaican Jimmy. Me beef is wit' da youth, but if me have ta go tru' ya ta splatta him, so be it," an evil, red-eyed Jagha said hostilely. He was more than willing to make good on his threat.

"Jagha, ya know good and well me can't do dat. Da bwoi, as ignorant as him may be, stilla part of me bloodline.

Now, wut he did wasn't called fa, and ya got every right ta leave him holier than thou, but me askin' ya, shotta to shotta, let da youth slide—just dis once. Do it as a fava fa me. If ya do, me owe ya big time."

Jagha thought on it for a minute. He loved to have nig-gaz indebted to him. He never knew when a favor could come in handy, especially given the lifestyle he'd chosen. "Awright, den," he said, putting the hammer of his blower back in place and lowering it. "But, da next time dis lil' muddafucka shoves a burna in me face, me will put 'em inna fuckin' box, ya undastand me, Jimmy? Hmmm?"

Jamaican Jimmy nodded understandingly and sheathed his katana. He signaled for his killaz to put away their guns, and they obeyed his command.

Jagha and Amoya put their blowers away also.

Fitzroy's eyes got as big as saucers seeing flickers of movement beyond the gates of the basketball court. He blinked his eyes, thinking that his mind was playing tricks on him. But that wasn't the case. Unfortunately for him, and the poor souls on the basketball court, by the time his brain registered what was going on, it was entirely too late.

Mack came through the gates first, off his bended knees, firing his mini Dracos. He knocked the bone structure and the meat out of Fitzroy's face. The young nigga spun around as he was met with gunfire. His limp body was in freefall when everyone else on the basketball court scattered like a cluster of mice. The people that gathered to see the game between Jagha and Fitzroy screamed and ran in a panic. They feared for their lives, and rightfully so. They were in the middle of a firefight.

Julian and Lil' Saint entered the gates of the basketball court behind Mack. Lil' Saint, clutching his Tec-9 with both gloved hands, lifted it up. He aimed it at Jagha and pulled the trigger. The semi-automatic weapon shook furiously in his hands. It spat rapid fire, and empty shell casings flew from it in a blur. A pained look swept over Jagha's face as he was chopped down and painted with his own blood. His eyes widened and his mouth flew open as he met with death. He crashed to the basketball court, releasing his sack and spilling his winnings.

Julian, scowling and clenching his teeth behind his ski mask, cut down the Rude Bwois in his sight with his AR-15. The screams and hollers of the men were so loud that they threatened to burst his eardrums. Seeing movement at the corner of his eye, Julian whipped around and found Amoya about to blow Lil' Saint's brains out. Swiftly, he swung his stick around and lit her tropical ass up like a Christmas tree. Amoya fell to her bloody demise wearing the face of death. Lil' Saint nodded his "thanks" to Julian for saving his ass, and Julian gave him a thumbs up. The two masked men charged forward to rejoin the gun battle at hand. While this was happening, innocent bystanders were running back and forth across them.

Seeing that the top dog's life was in danger, Jamaican Jimmy's bodyguards formed a wall in front of him. They cleared their guns from their waistlines and managed to get off a couple of shots. Unfortunately for them, their handguns weren't any match for the rapid fire of Mack's mini Dracos, which chopped their asses down.

Mack, Julian, and Lil' Saint exchanged heavy gunfire with the Rude Bwois. Mack caught two and went down, grimacing. Seeing their homeboy catch fire, Julian and Lil' Saint became heated. They turned the full fury of their guns on the Rastas and knocked them off their feet. They met their bloody end, lying on the basketball court bleeding, wearing that dead look on their faces.

"Okay, me see, ya wan' me head? Well, ya not gon' have an easy time gettin' it!" Jamaican Jimmy assured those that came to take his life. His face balled up begrudgingly. He slung his cobra-head staff to the ground, seeing as how it would be useless in a gunfight. Peeling off his overcoat, and then his suit's jacket, he pulled out two Glocks. He kept them on him for times like these. Having a security team was good, but he still needed to cover his own ass.

"Ya wan' rump wit' me, huh? Me show ya—me show ya howa real Rude Bwoi gets down fa his," Jamaican Jimmy said as he made his way toward the opposite side of the basketball court, with the panicked crowd. He had his two bangaz up and was letting both of them bitchez dance in his hands. The twin black guns ejected empty shell casings from one end and spat death from another. "Me top shotta, me Kingston's finest, ya hear me? Ya hear me, eh?" Jamaican Jimmy's braids bounced up and down on his shoulders as he backed up toward the exit of the basketball courts. His face was scrunched up, his teeth were sunk into his bottom lip, and he was spitting flames at his opps.

Bloc, Bloc, Bloc, Bloc, Bloc, Bloc!
Blowl, blowl, blowl, blowl!
Bloom, bloom, bloom!
Boc, boc, boc, boc!
"Aaaaaah!"
"Gaaaah!"
"Argggghhh!"

The Rude Bwois that were left screamed in excruciation as they fell to their demise. Jamaican Jimmy wasn't paying any attention to them, though. He was still getting busy with his Glocks, wolfing big shit. Although he was firing at the opposition, he was hitting innocent people that were trying to flee the chaos as well. Too bad for them, he didn't give a fuck! The way he looked at it, they were all casualties of war.

"Ya pwussy, alla ya pwussy," Jamaican Jimmy said, as he continued to bust his guns. He watched as Julian helped an injured Mack to his feet so they could flee, while Lil' Saint banged it out with them. Once Julian had gotten Mack to his feet, they hurried to make their escape while Lil' Saint laid down cover fire for them. Seeing his enemies retreating made Jamaican Jimmy's chest swell with pride and his nuts hang lower. "Dat's wright, batty bwois, run, run fa ya pathetic lives! Dis wut happens, ya see? Dis wut happens when ya rump witta god!" he went on popping shit and waving his warm, smoking guns around. At this time, police car sirens were wailing loudly in the distance heading to that very location. There were dead bodies and wounded people scattered on the basketball court. Those that were lucky enough to still have their lives were moaning and groaning in agony. They called out for help as their burgundy blood stained the pavement. The smell of gun smoke, blood, and death was heavy in the air.

Jamaican Jimmy reloaded his Glocks and started back busting at Mack, Julian, and Lil' Saint as they fled. Sparks flew off the gates, and they continued to retreat unscathed. The top dog was so busy sending heat at his enemies and talking shit, he neglected his surroundings. Unbeknownst to Jamaican Jimmy, a cold and calculating Hellraiser emerged from the shadows behind him. He moved with the stealth of a lioness on the hunt, creeping up behind him with murderous intent.

"Pwussy, pwussy bwois, ya not mon, ya beeches, pull ya skirt down!" Jamaican Jimmy said, watching Mack and them disappear into the darkness. It was funny to him how just a minute ago, the masked gunmen were busting at him and his crew. But now, they were retreating like a bunch of scared little girls. "Hahahahahahahahahahaha!" he threw his head back, laughing satanically. "Hahahaha—" Jamaican Jimmy's eyes exploded open and his mouth formed an O. Blood pooled inside of his grill and ran down his chin. He'd been blasted in his back. His spine felt like it was literally on fire. Making a 180-degree turn, he came face to face with a pair of evil eyes, staring at him through the openings of a ski mask. The top dog scowled and lifted both of his bangaz to lay down his assailant. But before he could pull his triggers, he was being blown away.

Bloom!

An explosion erupted out of the barrel of Hellraiser's shotgun, knocking off one of Jamaican Jimmy's dress shoes and sending him rocketing through the air. He landed hard on the asphalt, and his fedora flew off. He looked around like he was in a daze, coughing up blood, chest looking like it had been cut wide open for a surgical procedure. He was losing plasma fast, so his vision was coming in and out of focus. He was close to fainting and eventually dying. Realizing he was on his way out, he wanted to take his assassin with him. Pulling himself together as best as he could, he searched the grounds for his Glocks. He spotted one of them two feet away. It glinted underneath the lights of the basketball court.

"Uhhh," Jamaican Jimmy groaned as he turned onto his side, with slimy ropes of blood hanging from his chin. He began to crawl toward his gun. A smile slowly formed on his lips the closer he got to it. The palm of his hand was just about to grace the handle of the gun when a shadow eclipsed him and kicked it out of his reach. The Glock slid across the ground, spinning in circles and bumping against the lifeless form of one of the Rude Bwois.

Jamaican Jimmy looked up and swore he saw a dark, demonic figure towering over him. It had horns, huge bat-like wings, and the most terrifying pair of red eyes that seemed to glow like the flame of a lantern. Jamaican Jimmy knew that it was over for him. There wasn't any use of putting up a fight. His end was at hand. He shut his eyes and crossed himself in the sign of the holy crucifix. Shortly thereafter, the creature opened its mouth full of sharp, jagged teeth and unleashed a sweltering heat wave, annihilating his skull.

Bloom!

Jamaican Jimmy's head exploded, and what looked like Ragu sauce and chunks of hamburger flew everywhere. So much blood was pouring from out of his mutilated top that his cornrows looked like cooked spaghetti noodles drenched in tomato sauce.

Hellraiser lowered his smoking shotgun at his side and snatched the thick gold rope chain from Jamaican Jimmy's neck. It was speckled with his brain fragments and blood, but he didn't pay it any mind. He needed the piece of jewelry to confirm his slaying of the top dog to Caleb. Hearing a vehicle screeching to a halt behind him, Hellraiser whipped around and lifted up his shotgun, ready to lay any opposition down.

"Come on, babe!" Lachaun called out to him, waving him over from behind the wheel. Hellraiser looped Jamaican Jimmy's rope chain with the Jamaican flag on it over his neck and ran towards the van, hopping in. Before he could pull his foot inside and close the door, the van was speeding off.

Chapter Five

Hellraiser walked through the entrance of Bottoms Up. He stopped at the bar and scanned his surroundings. He was looking for one of Caleb's goons. When he didn't see any of the usual three cats he normally used, he pulled out his cellular to hit him up and see exactly who he was supposed to be linking up with. He was in the middle of texting him when he heard a familiar voice call his name from the depths of the establishment. When he looked up, he couldn't believe who he saw motioning for him to come over to his table. He deleted the message he intended to send to Caleb and stuck his cell phone into his pocket.

Caleb got all the jokes. He knows I don't fuck with this nigga, man. So, why'd he send 'em? Hellraiser thought as he approached the booth where Hitt-Man was sitting. Immediately, he sat his drink down and rose to his feet.

"What up, nigga?" Hitt-Man asked as he lifted his hand to greet Hellraiser.

Hellraiser looked at his hand like it was holding a rattlesnake in it. He then mad dogged him. "Bruh, if you don't knock it off. You know you and I"—he motioned a finger between them—"don't rock like that. Never have. Let's not start the fronting now."

Hitt-Man nodded understandingly and motioned for Hellraiser to sit down. Pulling up his jeans, he sat down and picked his drink back up. Hellraiser pulled out a black velvet pouch and passed it to Hitt-Man. He frowned, looking at it, wondering what it was. He looked up at Hellraiser and he insisted he take it. Hitt-Man took a quick sip of his drink, sat his glass down, and took the pouch. He opened it and pulled out Jamaican Jimmy's gold rope. It was gleaming in the lighting of the establishment. Hellraiser made sure he cleaned it up before he delivered it to whomever Caleb had in mind to send with his payment.

"Rest in shit, old nigga." Hitt-Man smiled as he looked at the gold rope. He then placed it back inside of the velvet pouch and stashed it inside his leather jacket. He then picked his drink back up and was about to take a sip, when he noticed Hellraiser hadn't sat down. "Relax. Pull up a chair. Take a seat, homeboy."

"I'd much rather get my check and go," Hellraiser told him straight up. "This isn't old fraternity brothers from college linking up, so there's no need for us to shoot the shit. You feel me?"

Hitt-Man took a sip of his drink and cleared his throat. He sat the glass down on the table top and leaned back in his seat. "You've already made that clear. I'd appreciate it if you kicked it for a few ticks, so we won't draw any suspicion to what we've got going."

Hellraiser scanned his surroundings and saw, though the establishment was scarce, there were nosy patrons stealing looks at them. He turned back to Hitt-Man and nodded. It was then he understood where he was coming from.

Hellraiser sat down, and Hitt-Man motioned the barmaid over. She was a light-skinned number with a small chest and a teardrop ass. Her physique made it apparent she worked out religiously. She was wearing a lace-front wig, long lashes, and a gold necklace with a tiny crucifix hanging from it. Little mama was heavily tattooed from her neck down to her wrists.

The barmaid stopped at Hellraiser and Hitt-Man's table, flipping open a small notepad. She held the small notepad in one hand and took her ink pen from behind her ear.

"Hey, handsome, what can I get cha?" she asked as she chewed gum and bounced her leg.

"Cranberry juice, sweetheart," Hellraiser replied.

"Cranberry juice?" the barmaid's brows furrowed as she questioned his request.

Hellraiser looked at her like, *Bitch, you heard exactly what I said.*

The barmaid shrugged and said, "Okay, cranberry juice it is." She didn't bother to write down his request as she walked away, closing her notepad.

"Tell me, how long you been fucking with Cal now?" Hitt-Man asked as he toyed with the red straw in his drink.

"A minute."

"Longer than me?"

"Nah, you've definitely known Cal longer than me."

"Here you go, handsome." The barmaid returned with Hellraiser's drink. She laid a napkin on the table top in front of him and sat his drink upon it.

"Thank you," Hellraiser said, taking a sip of his drink. She turned to walk away, but his calling her back stopped her in her tracks. He held up a twenty-dollar bill. "I guess you don't want cha tip." She went to take it, but he held fast. He looked at her. "What do you say?"

She smiled and said, "Thank you." Again, she went to leave with the money, but he held fast. She looked at him and he angled his head.

"Lil' mama, you forgot something?" Hellraiser told her with a raised eyebrow.

She smiled, looked to the side, and then back at him. "Thank you, handsome."

"That a girl." He smiled and released the twenty-dollar bill.

Smiling, she pocketed the money and walked away, throwing that booty from side to side. Hitt-Man watched as Hellraiser admired her ample bottom and massaged his chin.

"Ooooooh," Hitt-Man said like a little kid. "I'ma tell yo' boo yo' trifling ass was flirting with another bitch."

Hellraiser gave him a "whatever" face and waved him off. "Nigga, please, wifey know her nigga flirts from time to time. She'd doesn't give a fuck long as a nigga not dropping dick off in these broads." Hitt-Man nodded and took a sip of his drink.

"Which wifey would that be? Shaniqua or Lachaun?"

Hellraiser eyeballed him for what seemed like an eternity before he spoke again. "You know, Hitt-Man, I've always known you to be a macho asshole, but I never took you to be a nosy mothafucka." Hitt-Man cracked a grin. "Now, what were you getting at about Cal earlier?"

Hitt-Man held his glass in one hand while he stirred it with his straw. "Like you were saying beforehand, I've known boss dog longer than you have."

"What, chu holding my man's dick now?" Hellraiser asked and clapped his hands amusingly. "Good for you. Real fucking good for you."

"I don't hold anyone's dick. I'm my own man, Blood," Hitt-Man told him seriously. He looked to be offended by what Hellraiser had said to him. He had it in mind to shoot in his face, but his understanding of them not liking each other gave him pause. "All I'm telling you is, since I've known the homie longer, I know how he moves—what he's capable of. And it would be in your best interest to—"

Hellraiser's cellular's ringing interrupted Hitt-Man. He held up his finger and answered the call. "'Sup? Yeah, I'm finna come out now. Peace." He disconnected the call. "Yo, I've gotta go. Where that check at?"

Hitt-Man nodded downward, which meant underneath the table. Hellraiser grabbed it, hoisted his strap over his shoulder, and slid out of the booth. He downed the last of his drink and gave Hitt-Man a look. He didn't say goodbye, the nigga wasn't his homie. Fuck him!

"Yo, Hell!" Hitt-Man called after him. He stopped cold in his tracks and turned around to him. "Watch out for boss dog, fam—he's bad news!"

Hellraiser lifted his shirt so Hitt-Man could see his gun in his waistline. "So am I." He spun back around and walked off, shaking his head.

Fuck this nigga getting at? Is he tryna say Cal's looking to murk me? I seriously doubt that. My man's always been a standup nigga since we've been dealing. I mean, even if the homie was trying have me whacked, why the fuck would Hitt-Man be warning me? We don't even like each other! Blood, I've gotta be in the fucking Twilight Zone, Hellraiser thought as he disappeared through the exit door of the bar.

***

Da Crew decided to split up the money from the hit at Mack's crib. They sat around his dining room table chopping it up while Hellraiser ran the dead faces through a money counter. He made sure to separate the bread into five thousand-dollar stacks and sit them in their individual piles. Next, he pushed everyone's share in front of them. The bag was $150,000 dollars. Everyone got thirty gees apiece upon the completion of the assignment.

"This lick is one for the books, baby," Julian proclaimed as he kissed one of the rubberband stacks of money from his pile. He grabbed two more of the stacks, put them together, and used it as a telephone. "Lemme see what my nigga, Lil' Saint, doing." He punched imaginary buttons on the money. He held it to his ear and made a ringing sound.

Lil' Saint caught on quick and grabbed three stacks, treating them like a telephone also.

"That's the money calling, I betta pick up." Lil' Saint cracked a grin and held the stacks to his ear. "What up, nigga?"

Lil' Saint was a five-foot-six dark-skinned nigga who wore corrective lens eyeglasses. He wore his small afro in a taper fade and had a trimmed mustache. He looked dorky and was exceptionally quiet. He'd gotten the name Lil' Saint due to his short stature and his father being an ordained minister of a very prominent church.

Lil' Saint knew the Bible like he knew the back of his hand. If he had to, he could recite it backwards. Although his name was acquainted with holiness, the acts he committed were anything short of devilish. Lil' Saint and his old man, Minister Patrick Markham, used to work as hittaz for the Italian mafia. They were a couple of body snatchers who made their living shedding blood. It was well known that the little nigga was exceptionally talented with a gun. It was said he'd killed more people than the number of years he'd been alive. And although his father had quit the murder for hire game and given his life to doing God's work, Lil' Saint stayed in the mix and dedicated his life to doing the Devil's work.

Mack made a ringing sound as he held three stacks to his ear. "Awwww, shit, that's some more money calling. Lil' Saint, I think you better get that, Blood." Lil' Saint picked up some more stacks and held it to his other ear. "What up, niggaaaa?"

Right then, everyone in the dining room doubled over, laughing heartily.

"Yo, yo, this calls for a celebratory drink," Mack said, coming down from his laughter.

"What chu got us to drink on, my nigga?" Julian asked as he stacked up his earnings neatly.

"Cristal, my boy, if we're gonna celebrate, then we may as well do it in style," Mack said, removing his Kevlar bulletproof vest from off the dining room table.

"Sho' you right," Hellraiser chimed in and gave Lil' Saint a look. He nodded and glanced at his watch.

"Yo, let's make it quick, 'cause I gotta move I gotta make 'fore I take it in," Lil' Saint informed them.

"Fuck you going, lil' nigga? Santa has some gifts that's gotta be wrapped?" Julian inquired jokingly. Everyone busted up laughing, except Lil' Saint. He gave him the "Fuck you" finger.

"Man, all y'all can kiss my black ass," Lil' Saint said.

"Y'all leave my bro alone," Lachaun said, hugging and kissing Lil' Saint on the cheek.

"Lil mama," Mack addressed one of the sexy twins crowding him. One was massaging his shoulders while the other was sitting in his lap. She was applying ointment to the bruises he'd gotten when Jamaican Jimmy's bullets slammed into his bulletproof vest. "Go grab that bottle of Cristal outta the fridge and five champagne glasses for me."

"Okay, daddy," the twin massaging his shoulders said before turning to walk away.

"Hold up. Aren't you forgetting something?" Mack turned his cheek toward her and tapped his finger against it. She smiled as she walked back over to him and planted a wet one on him, leaving a lip gloss imprint kiss behind. As she walked away, he smacked her on her phat, round ass, and that mothafucka jumped. He admired her booty as she sauntered away, throwing that thang from side to side. "Mmmmmmunh," he said, thinking of how thick and sexy she was. There was no doubt in his mind that he was smashing her and her sister this night. "Make yo'self useful and go help yo' sister," he told the twin sitting on his lap. She capped the ointment, kissed him on his cheek, and hopped off his lap. He smacked her on her behind as she walked away as well.

When the twins returned, one of them had a gold bottle of Cristal while the other had the champagne glasses. A glass was placed on the table top in front of everyone that was a part of the crew. As soon as the glasses were placed on the table, the twin with the champagne came around, halfway filling them. Hellraiser told everyone to pick up their glass once he saw they were all full.

"Okay, I'd like to propose a toast to everyone involved in making this payday possible," Hellraiser began as he lifted up his glass of bubbly. Everyone followed behind him and held up their glasses as well. "If it wasn't for y'all—my friends, my brothers, my family, the love of my life." He looked at Lachaun and she blushed and smiled. "I couldn't have pulled this shit off tonight without y'all." He looked around the table at everyone's wrist as they held up their glass. "Da Crew" was inked there in Old English letters. "I love y'all—all of y'all, real shit—to Da Crew!"

"To Da Crew!" they said all together. They then touched glasses and sipped champagne.

Lil' Saint downed the rest of his champagne and sat his glass down on the table top. He loaded his share from the lick inside of his backpack and slipped its strap over his shoulder.

"Alright, y'all, I've gotta run," Lil' Saint told everybody. He went around the table exchanging "love yous" and performing their traditional handshake with them. Lachaun waved goodbye as he pulled open the door and disappeared through it. One of Mack's girls locked it behind him and returned to the table.

"So, what y'all niggaz plan on doing with y'all share of the loot?" Hellraiser inquired before taking another sip of champagne. Lachaun, who was sipping champagne also, was sitting on his lap with her arm around his shoulders.

"I was hollering at Old Man Griffith the other day. He's trying to sell Bottoms Up and retire," Julian told him. "I figure I'll take it off his hands."

"That's a good idea," Lachaun said.

"I've wanted to own my own bar since I wassa lil' nigga working in my granddaddy's juke joint back home," Julian told her.

"That's what's up, Blood. Good luck with that," Hellraiser said.

"Good looking out, bruh," Julian replied, tapping his fist to his chest.

"What about you, you pretty mothafucka?" Hellraiser looked at Mack. Now he had one twin massaging his shoulders while the other massaged his feet.

"I'ma open myself up a gentlemen's club, homie," Mack told him as he held his glass near his lips. "Give this pimping a new platform, if you know what I mean."

"That's a phenomenal idea, daddy," the twin massaging his feet told him.

"It definitely is, daddy. I think you should call it Club Mack Daddy," the twin massaging his shoulders said.

"Hmmmm." Mack looked off to the side while massaging his chin. He was thinking how the name of the club would look in neon green and blue lights at night. A smile spread across his lips. "Yeah, Club Mack Daddy, I fucks with that. That's just what I'ma call it, too."

"I don't give a fuck what you call it as long as I get up in that bitch free," Julian chimed in.

"I know that's right, bro," Lachaun said. "Me and my boo better be getting in that thang free of charge." She dapped up Julian.

"Hell naw, y'all some mothafucking criminals," Mack said with furrowed brows. "Y'all ghetto asses are sure to bring trouble. You definitely paying to enter my establishment. 'Cause I'ma have to cough up the extra dough for the top-notch security I'ma need." He took a sip of his champagne.

"Well, ain't this 'bouta bitch?" Hellraiser frowned and exchanged glances with everyone else. Everyone then looked at Mack, who was enjoying his massage and his champagne.

"What?" Mack said with a wrinkled forehead. He was wondering why they were eyeballing him.

"Nigga, yo' ass a criminal too!" everyone said in unison and launched stacks of money at him. Mack fell out of the chair but hopped back up laughing. He grabbed some of the money and started hurling it back at his crew along with his girls. The crew laughed and started hurling money back at him. It was like they were junior high school students having a food fight!

Laughter ran rampant throughout the dining room.

***

Lachaun was halfway up the street she lived on when she noticed someone hurrying away from her yard. He was wearing a cap, a jumpsuit, and toting what looked like a tool box to her.

"Hell's that coming outta my house?" a furrowed-brow Lachaun said and sat up in her seat.

76

"Where?" Hellraiser looked around, grabbing his gun.

"Right there! About to hop into that big white van," Lachaun pointed out the man in the cap and jumpsuit.

"Hop out and check on yo' crib. I'm on his ass, babe," Hellraiser told her as she pulled up in front of her house. She grabbed her gun, jumped out of the whip, and darted toward her house. He slid behind the wheel, slammed the door, and sped off.

***

Lachaun tucked her gun and opened her front door as fast as she could. She snatched open the iron door, then the wooden door, and rushed inside. Her eyes widened and she gasped. Instantly, her eyes overflowed with tears and spilled down her cheeks. Hearing footsteps behind her, she whipped around and couldn't believe who she saw behind her. Her knees buckled and she nearly collapsed.

"So, what's up, lil' mama? You tryna do this or what?" a smiling Hellraiser asked from a kneeling position. He was holding open a black ring box. It contained a yellow-gold engagement ring with a canary-yellow stone at its center. The ring cost an arm and a leg, but he didn't think twice about buying it. He felt his lady was well worth it, and then some.

Tears flooded Lachaun's cheeks as she said yes, and nodded rapidly. She pulled out her gun so it wouldn't dig into her hip as she got down on her knees. She kissed all over Hellraiser's face, tongued him down, and then wrapped her arms around his neck. She continued to cry as she held him.

"Oh, my god, babe, I love you. I love you so much," Lachaun swore.

"I love you too, lil' mama," Hellraiser replied. She broke her embrace and watched as he removed the ring from the box. She continued to cry and fan herself while he slipped the engagement ring onto her finger. It twinkled. She smiled, hugging and kissing him again.

Hellraiser scooped Lachaun into his arms and spun around. He kicked the door closed, and she reached past him to lock it. They kissed passionately as he carried her toward the bedroom. He made his way past dozens and dozens of big red roses before disappearing into the hallway. A huge banner was hanging over the hallway entrance. It had "Will you marry me?" on it.

"Babe, how'd you put this together?" Lachaun asked as he carried her down the hallway.

"Lil' Saint. Why you think he left so early?"

"Wait. So, that was him? The man in the cap and jumpsuit I saw leaving my house?"

"Yep. He lost the key to yo' place that I gave 'em so he had to work his magic to get in," Hellraiser told her as he turned the corner inside of her bedroom. "You know that nigga works as a locksmith for his pops and shit. Anyway, he got in and set this up for me."

"When did you find time to get my ring?" Lachaun asked. She couldn't take her eyes off of it. She loved it. It was amazing!

"I've been sitting on that thang for a while now."

"Well, I love it. It's absolutely gorgeous," she admitted, hugging him and kissing him once more. "I don't know how to thank you."

"Well, I can think of one way." He looked at her and smiled. She smiled back, cupped his face, and kissed him.

"Oh, you most def' gon' get it once I get out this shower," Lachaun assured him once he'd sat her down. "Come on, big daddy." She grabbed his wrist and led him inside of the bathroom. They stripped until they were as naked as Adam and Eve. They then showered, washing each other and then rinsing off.

Hellraiser stepped out of the tub to leave Lachaun to wash her hair. The entire bathroom was foggy, and the medicine cabinet mirror was cloudy. He snatched the towel off the rack and dried himself off. He returned to the bedroom where he applied deodorant and rubbed on a scented oil he'd bought from a Muslim brother posted up at the Baldwin Hills shopping plaza. He'd just stepped his bare foot inside of a pair of Fruit of the Loom boxer briefs when he heard Lachaun behind him.

"There's no needa you putting them on, you're gonna end up taking them back off, anyway," Lachaun said, drawing his attention over his shoulder. He tossed his underwear aside and turned around to his fiancée. She'd emerged from the bathroom wearing nothing more than a towel, with fog rolling out behind her. Her hair was long and wet from her showering. There were beads of water peppered over her shoulders and chest. "You ready for this pussy, daddy?"

"Oh, yes, big daddy ready for all that's underneath that towel," Hellraiser said confidently. He could feel his dick bricking up. Lachaun was as much of a G as he was, so her naturally being feminine and submissive really got him going. He licked his lips sexily as he rubbed his hands together in anticipation of the sex she'd bestow upon him.

Lachaun smiled, seeing she had her fiancé's undivided attention. She could tell by the hunger in his eyes that he was craving her like a crackhead did rocks for his pipe. It felt good to be wanted by someone that she wanted just as bad. She wanted to get real freaky for her boo and be his naughty little slut for the night. All she could think about was fulfilling his every sexual desire and being conquered in submission by him. The thought alone made her so wet that she trickled onto the carpet. She could tell by Hellraiser's semi-erect dick he was aroused too.

Lachaun released her towel, and it fell in a pile at her feet. Hellraiser's eyes exploded open, and his mouth flung open. His reaction was like he'd never seen her naked before. He took her in from head to toe. He couldn't help thinking how he'd gotten so lucky every time they were alone. Shorty looked delicious to him. He could literally eat her up. All five-foot-nine inches of her! She was built like the Amazon warriors of the West African Dahomey Kingdom. Little mama was undoubtedly a bad bitch, but he'd never disrespect her with that word. Nah, she was his queen, and she deserved to be sitting beside his throne—like she was supposed to be—forever.

Chapter Six

"Come here," Lachaun called Hellraiser over, curling and uncurling her French tip-nailed finger. The smile on Hellraiser's face grew broader and broader the closer he got to her. His muscular, vein-riddled body and rock-hard abs were on full display. His dick slung from left to right, hitting his thighs with each step he took. He took her by the waist and she threw her arms around his neck. She looked in his eyes and they opened their mouths. Their tongues flicked back and forth across each other. He started sucking her tongue like it was an apple Jolly Rancher. Next, he sucked all over her lips and she tilted her head back. Her eyelids fluttered whiteness and she could feel her pussy getting wetter. He bit softly around her chin and trailed the tip of his tongue alongside the vein going down her neck. Halfway down, he gently bit into it and she gasped, loving the sensation it brought her. He traced her collarbone with his tongue and slid it up and down between her breasts. Her areolas were two shades darker and the nipples of them poked out. They were hard and begging to be sucked.

Hellraiser's strong, vein-riddled hands grabbed Lachaun's tits and mashed them together. She closed her eyes and caressed his cornrows as he traced her areolas with his tongue. He flicked her nipples, giving them their worth in attention. He bit down gently on them and pulled them softly. The action caused a chill to slide up Lachaun's back and her legs to wobble. She loved to have her nipples manipulated. She loved it even more when they were sucked. With knowledge of this, Hellraiser mashed her breasts as close together as he could and took turns sucking on each of them. He moaned as he feasted on her ample bosom.

reached the stubble of his mound when an avalanche of hot saliva spilled out of her mouth. The fifty-degree fluid slid down his shaft and coated his shaved nutsack.

Lachaun slowly slid her mouth up and down Hellraiser's dick while jerking it at the same time she was rubbing her love button. She was "mmmmmming" as she sucked on him, treating his shit like it was a melting cherry pineapple Big Stick Popsicle.

"Sssssss, fuck!" Hellraiser's nostrils flared, he grunted, and his top lip peeled back in a snarl. The veins in his forehead and neck became pronounced. He bit his inner jaw and began humping into her mouth. "Yeah, yeah, yeah, just like that, mamas! Handle yours, sucka nigga dick! Ahhhhh!" His eyes narrowed and he threw his head back. He placed his hands on the top of her head and started fucking her mouth like it was a warm, wet, dripping pussy.

Lachaun closed her eyes and held his muscular, hairy thighs as he fucked her mouth. Her face balled up as she gagged and coughed around his piece. Her saliva oozed from around her mouth and hung in slimy strings.

"Ack, ack, ack, ack, ack!" Lachaun continued to gag and choke on her boo's dick. She was letting him go as far inside of her mouth as he wanted. At the same time, she continued to rub on the small piece of meat between her sex lips while massaging his nutsack. His moaning was like a sexual stimulant for her. More and more of her essence spilled from between her thighs and dripped onto the floor.

"Mmmmm—uh, uh, uh—uh, uh—mmmmm, shit!" Hellraiser moaned and fucked her mouth viciously. The friction his head felt at the back of her throat was teasing him with a nut. It drove him to go for broke, stroking her mouth like a mad man. "Dammmmn, ah, I feel it! I feel it, babe!

This mothafucka 'bouta bust, it's 'bouta bust, mamas! Yeah, yeah—here I cum!" he grunted and swallowed his spit.

"Cum—cum—cum for me, daddy, cum for me!" Lachaun was trying to say with a mouthful of her man's meat. She didn't know how, but her nigga understood her every word and it drove him to do just that.

"Ahhhhh, you sexy, nasty, chocolate mothafucka!" Hellraiser's eyes popped back open and he looked down at Lachaun, who was looking up at him. He held one hand out at his side while the other rested on top of her head. He pushed his shit in and out of her mouth as he unleashed a nice, creamy load inside of her mouth. He continued to pump her mouth as beads of sweat oozed out of his forehead and ran down his face. The more semen he fed her, the more she swallowed, with his dick still in her mouth. His shit was pulsating in her grill. He left it in there until he was sure she'd gotten every last drop out of him.

Hellraiser slowly inched his piece out of Lachaun's mouth. She stayed on her knees with her mouth open so he could see his nut cupped in her tongue. She took her fingers from between her legs and showed them to him. They were glistening wet with speckles of her cum on them. She kept her mouth open and let him watch her swallow his babies as if they were an Advil.

Hellraiser smiled and wiped the sweat from his forehead. "Wheww, that shit was alla that," he proclaimed and helped Lachaun to her feet. With blinding speed, his hand flew out and latched around her neck, aggressively. He walked her back until she bumped into the bed. A smile spread across her face. She felt her kitty getting wet all over again.

Hellraiser licked and sucked on Lachaun's juicy lips. He then kissed her long, deep, and hard. In the middle of them making out, he parted her legs and slipped his middle finger inside of her. Her hole was hot and gooey. He added another finger and his thumb to the equation, so as he fingered her, his thumb would rub against her clit. He built up speed as he finger-fucked her, curled fingers hitting her spot. As he began to speed up his fingering, she made blissful faces and moaned between their lips. After a while, it got so good she put her foot on the bed. She tilted her head back, gasping and humping forward into his hand.

"Uh, uh, uh, uh, uh!" Lachaun moaned and whined, feeling an orgasm building between her thighs. Hellraiser swept his tongue up and down the vein on the side of her neck. He gently bit up its length then sucked on it as he fingered her feverishly.

"Mmmmm, you like that, baby?" Hellraiser asked between sucking on her neck.

"Y-yes, don't stop, daddy! P-please—don't stop—I'm 'bouta cum! I'm 'bouta fucking cum!" Lachaun swore as she tilted her head further back and allowed him to bite softy into her throat. His licking, sucking, and fingering her all at the same time had her legs buckling. She nearly fell a couple of times but righted herself at the last minute. She kept humping into his hand as he finger-fucked her, matching his rhythm. "Ooooh, shiiiiiit!" Her eyes bulged and she looked down at his hand. His fingers were moving in and out of her so fast that they looked like a blur. Her eyes bulged further and her mouth hung open, displaying all her teeth. "I'm cuming! I'm—I'm cum—cumiiiiiing!" she said while looking him dead in his eyes. His face was balled up and he was smiling at her fiendishly. The look on his face told her, *Yeah, bitch, I'm the mothafucking man, and this my pussy!*

"You 'bouta cum, huh? You 'bouta make daddy's pussy cum?" Hellraiser asked as he bit down hard on his bottom lip and fingered her that much faster.

"Ooooh—yesssssss!" Lachaun screamed and threw her head back. Her eyes rolled back to the white and her mouth hung further open. She shook crazily as her natural juices spurted and then sprayed out of her. She soaked Hellraiser's hairy thigh, leg, and foot. He smiled harder, looking at what he'd done. Still holding her by the neck, he kissed her in the mouth and then pushed her ass back on the bed. Her pussy was jumping and constantly spurting her secretions. Her eyes were still at their whites and her mouth was still hanging open. She was shaking so goddamn hard he thought she'd rise straight up into the air, on sorcery type shit.

Lachaun lay on the bed breathing hard and staring up at the ceiling. She couldn't move an inch. It was like she was paralyzed from cuming so hard. Hellraiser looked at her while stroking his meat up and down. Her pussy was oozing and contracting. He could see pink insides, and it turned him on. His dick felt like it doubled in size while in his hand.

"Look at that pretty-ass pussy, it's leaking like a busted faucet," Hellraiser declared as he stepped closer between her legs. "I done bust this bitch wide open. Son of a bitch fits me like a glove." He sucked on his two fingers so they'd be wet enough to do what he had in mind. He pressed his fingertips down on her sensitive clitoris and she jumped, startled. He then rubbed her clit back and forth really fast. Lachaun opened her legs wide like she was about to push out a baby. Her eyes fluttered as she forced her head back into the bed and smacked a pillow over her face. She screamed loud as fuck into it, meeting her second orgasm. She involuntarily sprayed him with her clear fluid again before going limp. Lachaun lay on the bed, looking like she'd die in a minute.

moment. He smacked each of Lachaun's buttocks back to back. It both stung and turned her on at the same time. She came again, wagging her butt and licking her top lip. Her twat was contracting and oozing with more of her secretions. She was dying to feel her man deep within her sacred valley.

"Damn, babe, you fiending for this dick, huh? That pussy gushy as fuck," Hellraiser said, marveling at her moist, pulsating treasure. "You know what? I want chu to lie on yo' back right here." He grabbed one of the pillows and placed it at the center of the bed. He instructed her how to lie on the pillow. His reason was for him wanting to have a good angle to get deep up in her.

Lachaun laid her lower back on top of the pillow, which made her ass be propped up. Hellraiser crawled into bed, lifted her leg, and laid it on his shoulder. He slid the head of his dick up and down her slit teasingly. She moaned and whined her hips. He tapped his piece against her sensitive clit, driving her crazy! Her body was on fire for him. She not only wanted him, she needed him—desperately.

"Baby, if you don't stop playing with my pussy and fuck me, I'ma bite cho ass. I'm horny as shit! And I wanna be fucked silly," Lachaun claimed with her eyes shut, spreading the delicate buds of her flower. He could see her phat pussy in all of its heavenly glory, and he couldn't wait to feel her walls.

"You know when you talk that nasty shit to me it turns me on, right? I'ma nail yo' lil' ass to the mothafucking cross." Hellraiser smiled devilishly, and she tugged on his piece, making semen ooze out of it. His shit got stronger and started jumping in her hand.

"Ummmhmmm." Lachaun nodded to his question, continuously tugging on him. "Ooooou, him ready for phat ma, huh? Him want some of this pussy?" The corner of her lips curled into a smile. "I want chu to choke me like you were when you were fingering me, daddy. This time, I want chu to do it hard, though. Choke me and fuck me hard, gimme some of that thug passion."

"Oh, yeah, that's what chu want?" Hellraiser snarled and smacked her across the face, leaving a red hand impression behind.

"Yessss!"

"Huh?"

Hellraiser smacked her again, but this time it was on the opposite cheek. It was stinging red with his hand impression also. The shit aroused her even more, making that pussy jump and ooze again.

"Ooooou, yes, daddy! Yes, yes, yes!" Lachaun called out, rubbing her clit in a circular motion. She nearly came when she felt his hand grip her at the neck. "Ack, ack, tighter—ack, tighter, dad—daddy—y—yeah, that's it." She rubbed her clit in a circular motion even faster.

Keeping one of his hands locked around Lachaun's throat, Hellraiser spat on the fingers of his freehand and rubbed his saliva around the head of his dick. He placed himself at his fiancée's entrance and eased himself inside of her. He sank inside of her, and they both gasped. Her eyes fluttered and her mouth stretched wide. He was saying 'damn' and 'fuck' under his breath with his eyes closed. He bit down on his bottom lip and shook his head. He couldn't believe how amazing she felt. No matter how many times he got some of her jewel, he'd never get used to how perfectly she fit him. Her shit was slick, snug, and hot—98.6°F to be exact. And he loved every bit of it.

"Oh, yeah, this my shit—this my mothafucking pussy," Hellraiser growled as he slowly stroked her in a circular motion, giving her half the dick with each plunge.

Tranay Adams

Chapter Seven
Morning

Once Shaniqua finally regained consciousness, her head and stomach were killing her. She'd fought Hellraiser plenty of times in the past, but he'd never put his hands on her. Normally, he'd let her hit him until she wore herself out, or he'd leave the apartment to give her time to calm down. But not this time! Nah, this time she was in for a rude awakening!

Shaniqua had blown up Ruby and Hellraiser's phones, but they weren't answering them. She left messages on them until she couldn't leave any more, and then she smashed her cellphone in a fit of rage. She pulled out her gun where she kept it inside of a case in the back of the closet and headed to the bathroom.

Shaniqua stood before the medicine cabinet mirror, looking at her pitiful reflection. Her hair was a mess, her eyes were red webbed, and there was yellowish-green crust at the corners of them. Her top lip and chin were drenched with a mixture of tears and snot. Her mind was assaulted by a barrage of suicidal thoughts. They hit her back to back and overwhelmed her. She needed an escape from her life. She desperately wanted to die!

"Fuck this shit! I'm so tired of this shit. I'm so fucking tired of it!" Shaniqua broke down in the mirror, sobbing and shuddering. "Living hurts. It hurts so bad, I just wanna be at peace. I just wanna escape."

Shaniqua squeezed her eyes shut and stuck the cold black gun inside her mouth. She bit down on the metal, and that's when she knew it was real. She was really about to take her own life. She squeezed her eyes shut tighter, and more tears spilled.

guardrail as she descended the staircase. She closed both doors of the house and darted out onto the front lawn. A mad dog look was on her face as she stared up at the house, holding her gun at her side. Suddenly, she lifted and pointed her gun. She pulled the trigger and put holes in the mailbox. Then, she shot out all the windows of the house, shattering the glass. Satisfied with her handiwork, she put her gun back in its hiding place inside the trunk and peeled off.

I know where his ass at. He's laid up with that bitch and my mothafucking baby playing house. This ho, Lachaun, think she gon' cut me outta the picture so she can take my family and live happily ever after. Nuh unh, she got me fucked up! KiMani is my child! Treymaine is my man! I don't give a fuck if we broke up or not! Once mine, always mine, Shaniqua thought as she raced down the residential street.

***

Shaniqua whipped past a teal '00 Chrysler 300M, leaving dust particles going up in the air and drifting down to the paved road. Ruby slid up from the driver's seat and peered into the sideview mirror. She watched as Shaniqua's vehicle continued speeding down the block until its back lights disappeared. A worried look was on her face, and she rifled through her purse for her cellular to tell Hellraiser what she'd seen.

"Grandma Ruby, who are you hiding from?" KiMani asked from the backseat where he was strapped in a car seat. He had a wet, sticky mouth and a popsicle in his hand. He was oblivious to the fact that his grandmother had just watched his mother break into her home and shoot out all of its windows.

"No one, baby," Ruby replied with a lie as she scrolled through her contacts for Hellraiser's number. Once she pressed the 'call' button and the line started ringing, she placed the cellular to her ear. She looked at the sideview mirror again for Shaniqua's car to see if she was coming back, but she didn't see it. The line continued to ring as she drummed her fingers on the steering wheel.

Come on, come on. Pick up, pick up, pick up, Ruby thought with worrisome eyes and a thudding heart. She didn't know for sure, but something told her that Shaniqua was out of her mind and looking to body Lachaun and her son.

She was positive Shaniqua would have murdered her and her grandson, if they had been home. Luckily, she decided to go grocery shopping, so she wasn't there. She thanked the Lord she'd gotten up that morning when she did. She'd had it in mind to make a nice breakfast and spend the day watching cartoons with her grandson.

***

Urrrrrk! Craaaash!

Two automobiles crashed head-on at the intersection as Shaniqua made an illegal turn at a traffic light. She zipped up the block with the hand of the speedometer coming around fast as she whisked past vehicles on both sides of the street. A look of determination was in her eyes, and thoughts were racing through her mind once again.

"Bitch gotta 'notha thang coming if she think she's gonna take what's rightfully mine. That's my family—my goddamn family! Grrrr!" Shaniqua's face twisted into something out of a horror movie, and she slammed her fist into the dashboard.

99

with. She was thirsty for blood, but not just anyone's blood—Lachaun's blood!

"Shaniqua, stop this shit before someone gets—Ahhhh, fuck!" Hellraiser's eyes bulged, and he hollered. He looked to his arm and she'd sliced him. Blood was sliding down his arm fast. He looked back up at her and saw her swinging the shard again. He threw his forearm up and grimaced. A burning sensation engulfed his arm as she sliced him again. He whipped around to shield Lachaun, dropping his gun in the process. "Aaaahhh!" he threw his head back, hollering as fire shot across his back. Shaniqua had sliced him once again.

Lachaun shoved Hellraiser to the floor, leaving herself vulnerable to Shaniqua's attack. She moved with the agility of a cat avoiding the shard, but she was eventually sliced across the arm.

"Aaahhhh!" Lachaun hollered out and smacked her hand over her bleeding wound. When Shaniqua got her first taste of blood, she went into a frenzy like a shark. She came harder and faster at Lachaun. Lachaun moved swiftly, avoiding her advances. She ducked Shaniqua as she swung the shard toward her face. Lachaun sprang back up, back-hand punching her, and then kicking her in the chest. Shaniqua dropped the bloody shard as she rocketed across the living room. She grunted as her back slammed against the wall and caused a portrait of Lachaun and Hellraiser to fall. The glass of the portrait cracked as it hit the floor and fell facedown.

"Uhhhh," Shaniqua moaned as she sat slumped against the wall. Her back was sore, and she felt a migraine coming on. She winced as she looked up and saw Lachaun in a martial arts fighting stance. She had fire in her eyes, her top lip was peeled back in a sneer, and she was ready to defend herself should Shaniqua launch another attack.

"That's enough, goddamn it! Y'all stop this shit!" Hellraiser yelled from the floor, bleeding from his cuts. Just then, his cellular stopped ringing. Three seconds later, it started back up ringing again. For the fifth time, he didn't answer it!

"Nah, it's over when she says it's over," Lachaun replied, keeping her eyes on Shaniqua. "So, is it over?"

Shaniqua frowned and clenched her teeth. A low growl slowly built up from the depths of her stomach, and she balled her hand into a fist. She looked to the portrait of Lachaun on the wall with her sensei after winning a championship match. She realized then that she'd never stand a chance against her.

"Fuck this shit!" Shaniqua spat furiously and slammed her fist down on the carpeted floor. She then pointed her bloody finger at Lachaun threateningly. "I've got heat for bitchez like you!" She jumped to her feet, opened the front door, and charged out of it.

Hellraiser's cellular started ringing again. Its ringing was driving him crazy, so he looked at its display. It was Hitt-Man again! He had a total of six missed calls, and they all came from him. He pressed the ignore button and slipped the cell phone back into his pocket.

"I see this bitch can't take an ass whipping," Lachaun said to no one particular. At the exact same time, she and Hellraiser zeroed in on the gun he'd dropped. He realized then that she was going to use it to pop Shaniqua before she popped her. Hellraiser crawled toward the gun as fast as he could while Lachaun dove for it. She landed the closest to it, grabbed it, turned over onto her back and checked its magazine. Once she saw it was fully loaded, she smacked the clip back in and cocked it. She then hurried to her feet and made fast tracks out of the front door. Hellraiser was right behind her, leaving a trail of blood behind him.

"Baby, no!" Hellraiser called after her as he met the outside. He squinched his eyes from the intense rays of the sun. He could see Lachaun going after Shaniqua, who was standing at her opened trunk. A moment later, she pulled out a gun of her own, and she and Lachaun exchanged gunfire.

Bloc, bloc, bloc!

Poc, poc, poc!

Hellraiser threw his arms over his head as he zig zagged, trying to avoid the deadly exchange. A bullet whizzed by his ear. He dove to the ground and avoided another bullet that slammed into an enormous tree behind him. Lying on his stomach, while Lachaun and Shaniqua's gun battle was taking place, he looked up the block to see an Astro van speeding in their direction.

Hellraiser looked back and forth between Lachaun and Shaniqua. Lachaun was treading back to her house while Shaniqua was taking shots at her from behind the cover of her whip. The Astro van was coming up fast, and its side door was sliding open even faster. In fact, once the van's sliding door was fully opened, a masked gunman came into view. He was wearing a ski mask and all-black attire. His gloved hands gripped a Tec-9.

Hellraiser's eyes nearly popped out of his head seeing the danger they were all in. He shouted for his fiancée and his baby mama to stop and pointed at the gunman. Time seemed to slow down to a snail's pace then. All he could hear was his heart beating faster and faster, alongside the ringing of his cell phone. The gunman was halfway up the street by now. Hellraiser was up on his feet and sprinting toward Lachaun. She was the closest woman to him, so he had a better chance at saving her life in time.

"Getttt dowwwwnn!" Hellraiser yelled as he dove across the air to tackle Lachaun to the ground. He collided with her, and they crashed to the front lawn. Her gun flew up in the air and landed five feet away from her.

Hellraiser and Lachaun looked up at the van from where they lay on the ground. The masked gunman was spraying his Tec-9 with a vengeance. Shaniqua went to turn around and return fire. She'd turned halfway around before bullets lit her ass up!

"Noooooo!" Hellraiser called out to her and outstretched his hand.

"Ahhhhh!" Shaniqua threw her head back, screaming in pain as the hot bullets burned her form. She fell awkwardly to the ground and dropped her gun.

The gunman set his sights on Hellraiser and Lachaun, continuing his relentless firing. A line of bullets pelted the ground in front of them and sent dirt clouds into the air. Hellraiser lowered his and Lachaun's heads to the lawn to avoid the gunfire.

Hellraiser's cellphone started back ringing again!

The time sped back up to its normal pace!

The gunman slid the van's door closed, and the vehicle sped down the block. Hellraiser's head popped up. He looked to a bleeding and blood-gurgling Shaniqua. Then, he scanned his surroundings and spotted his gun. Furious, he crawled fast to his piece, like a gorilla, and picked it up. He ran out into the middle of the street, lifted his blower, and pulled its trigger like a mad man!

Poc, poc, poc, poc, poc, poc!

Hellraiser fired his gun until the van became an ant before his eyes. He lowered his smoking gun at his side and continued to watch the van. Taking a deep breath, he walked in Shaniqua's direction. He was breathing heavily, and his heart was racing. His vision became obscured from the water filling his eyes, and he sniffled. He wiped his nose with the back of his hand as he neared Shaniqua. He found her lying on her back. Her eyes were wide and her mouth was moving animatedly. Blood overflowed her mouth, and some of it got on her bloody shirt.

"Yes, I'd like to report a shooting," Lachaun said as she walked up on Hellraiser. Tears were pouring out of his eyes, and he was holding Shaniqua in his arms. His cellphone rang as she gave the dispatcher their location and disconnected the call. "Babe, gimme yo' gun and hers so I can put 'em up." Hellraiser handed her both of the guns. Afterward, he continued to hold Shaniqua in his arms and looked down into her fearful eyes.

"Fight it! Fight that shit, lil' mama! Come on now, fight! Fight with everything you've got," Hellraiser told her as he rocked her back and forth. The tears poured down his cheeks, and a snot bubble manifested in his right nostril. Shaniqua was staring up at him wide-eyed while gurgling on blood. The blood filled up in her mouth and ran out the corners of her lips. Her bloody hand grasped his hand, and she looked like she was fighting to stay alive. "That' s right, fight! Fight it—you've gotta—you've gotta—Aaahhhh!" Hellraiser made an ugly face as he rocked back and forth. He looked down into Shaniqua's dying eyes, and her mouth was moving slower and slower. Soon, her grasp on his hand became weaker and weaker.

Police car and ambulance sirens filled the air.

Hellraiser looked over his shoulder and saw Lachaun running out of the house. His cellular was ringing this entire time, but he chose not to answer it yet. He looked to Shaniqua's face and saw she was still breathing. He was still scared for her, but he was grateful she was still alive. That meant there was still a chance to save her life.

The cell phone stopped ringing. Then it started right back up!

"Where the fuck is this goddamn ambulance, man?" Hellraiser's head was on a swivel looking for the ambulance. He pulled out his cellphone and saw it was Hitt-Man again. He figured it must have been serious since he'd been blowing up his jack. He took the time to compose himself as best as he could before taking the call.

"Y—yeah? What's up?" Hellraiser said into his cellphone.

"Blood, I've been blowing you up! Fuck you at?" Hitt-Man said into the phone. He sounded like he was in dire need to warn him about something sinister. "I just got word that Cal's sending a hit squad to take you out."

The news hit Hellraiser like a punch to the gut. He was stunned. His cellphone slipped out his hand, and he bawled his eyes out. He felt that if he would have answered Hitt-Man's call sooner, then he could have possibly avoided Shaniqua's execution.

"Hello? Hell? Hell? Hell, are you there, man?" Hitt-Man's voice came from the cellphone.

A sorrowful Lachaun kneeled beside Hellraiser. She wrapped her arm around his neck and laid her head against his. Although she didn't care about Shaniqua, she did care about the pain her death brought her man. Right then, people began to emerge out of their homes to see what was going on. A minute later, the police and ambulance drove up.

Chapter Eight
Night

Hitt-Man paced back and forth in front of a garage smoking a cigarette. He'd spoken to Hellraiser an hour ago, and he'd informed him of Shaniqua's passing. Although he'd never been in his shoes, he could only imagine how fucked up he was behind her death. He and Hellraiser were some head busters that would go all out behind their loved ones. So, he knew he was about to be on some real murder shit behind this situation. He could hear that shit in his voice when he hit him up from the hospital.

Hitt-Man gave Hellraiser the address where he was to meet him. The address belonged to one of Caleb's spots out in Compton. The place was on 124th and Compton Avenue, dead smack in the hood! This was where Caleb often went to lay low and get his mind right with a bad bitch or two. No one outside of the top dog and Hitt-Man knew about this location. Although Caleb didn't trust a mothafucking soul, his relationship with Hitt-Man was different than the one he had with anyone else. They had a brotherly bond and considered each other family. They shared everything with one another—something that may play a role in Caleb's demise.

Hitt-Man stopped his pacing when he was overwhelmed by the headlights of an oncoming vehicle coming up the driveway. His eyes narrowed into slits, and he held his gloved hand above his brows to see who it was. He couldn't make them out, so he dropped his cigarette at his foot and mashed it out. He then pulled his gun from the small of his back and held it at the back of his leg. Should whomever driving up be there on behalf of Caleb to whack him, then he was going out like a G behind his—straight up!

113

The illumination from the headlights vanished and re-vealed the whip it belonged to: a big ass Chevrolet Suburban. It was black. It also had limousine-tinted windows. The passengers could see out, but no one could see inside. This was the perfect ride to creep up on a nigga and lay him down. With that in mind, Hitt-Man swung his gun around, ready to fire. He was about to start busting until he got a text. Still pointing his gun, he pulled out his cellular to see who it was hitting him up.

Hellraiser: Relax! It's just us.

Us? I thought I told this nigga to come solo, Hitt-Man thought as he lowered his gun and put his cellphone away.

The doors of the Chevrolet Suburban popped open, and Hellraiser and his crew hopped out. There was Lil' Saint, Julian, Mack, and Lachaun. They were all dressed in black and wearing gloves over their hands. Their faces and demeanors were as serious as a cancer diagnosis. Hellraiser led the pack as they approached Hitt-Man. Hellraiser was smoking a cigarette, which he flicked aside. Hitt-Man could tell he'd been crying from his red-webbed eyes and dry tears on his face.

"What's this?" a frowning Hitt-Man asked with his arms spread apart. He looked over all the faces of Hellraiser's crew.

"My family," Hellraiser said as he blew smoke from his nose and mouth.

"That's right. My nigga not going nowhere by himself, especially with all this shit going on," Mack said seriously.

"That's right," Lil' Saint began, adjusting his eyeglasses. "You fuck with one of us, then you're fucking with all of us."

"All for one and one for all, dog," Julian chimed in as he stepped beside Mack.

"All for one and one for all? Fuck are you niggaz? The Three Musketeers or some shit?" Hitt-Man asked with hostility. He didn't want so many ears present for fear of Caleb finding out his involvement in the move they were about to make. "Blood, you've gotta head hard as a rock," he told Hellraiser as he shook his head disappointedly. He then tucked his gun at the small of his back.

"So, what's up? What chu call me here for?" Hellraiser asked as Lachaun interlocked her fingers with his.

"Caleb wasn't just coming for yo' head, he was going for those of your crew as well," Hitt-Man told him as he removed the wrapper from a blue-raspberry Tootsie Roll pop. His news had Hellraiser and his crew exchanging confused glances.

"Wait a minute, you mean to tell me this cocksucka is sending a hit squad for us too?" Julian frowned. Hitt-Man nodded nonchalantly as he sucked on his sucker.

"I don't understand," Lachaun finally spoke. "What's this mothafucka's deal? I mean, why is he tryna have us all whacked?"

Hitt-Man pulled the sucker out of his mouth and licked his lips. "You know that hit y'all carried out against the Rude Bwoi posse? Well, he's tryna eliminate everyone that can tie 'em to that shit. So, that means all parties involved gotta go."

"Bitch-ass nigga!" Mack growled angrily and kicked the side of the Suburban, denting it.

"Hold up," Lil' Saint started back up. "We've carried out several jobs for Caleb in the past. Why is it now that he wants to have us clipped after this particular one?"

"That's what I wanna know," Julian said, folding his arms across his chest.

"Me too," Lachaun threw in her two cents.

"This one is on an entirely different level, homeboys and homegirl," Hitt-Man said before going on to divulge more information. "That set of Rude Bwois y'all blew off the map wassa minute fraction of their chapter. Them lil' dread-head fuckaz running around"—he motioned around with his sucka—"gotta army that's a lil' over five thousand strong throughout So Cal. That's not including the reinforcements they can call in from the island when shit kicks off out here. Yeah, Caleb's gotta army fulla die hard niggaz and whatnot. But it's not near enough to bump heads with these curry chicken-eating mothafuckaz." He stuck the sucker back in his mouth and started sucking it again.

Hellraiser and his crew nodded their understanding. Hitt-Man was spitting the truth. Caleb did have a lot of gully mothafuckaz riding with him, but a small army against thousands wouldn't stand a chance.

"Yo, so, when is he 'pose to send these hittaz at the rest of us?" Mack asked curiously.

"Tonight," Hitt-Man replied. "But chu don't have any-thing to worry about. I took care of that."

"You? By yo' damn self?" Mack inquired. He had a look on his face like he didn't believe him.

Hitt-Man nodded and motioned for them to follow him with his sucker. He made his way over to the side door of the garage. Mack, Julian, and Lil' Saint pulled out their guns as they followed behind them. Although they felt Hitt-Man was being on the up and up, they still didn't trust him.

Hitt-Man unlocked the side door of the garage and pulled it open. It was dark inside.

"Y'all, come in!" Hitt-Man called out to them. No one dared to walk inside of the garage until he flipped on the light switch. The crew spilled inside of the garage little by little. The first thing they saw was an off-white, black-tinted window Astro van.

Hitt-Man pulled open the sliding door of the Astro van. There were a total of six bloody, bullet-riddled goons with flies swarming around them. The smell of gunpowder, blood, and shit caused everyone to frown and look away. They made disgusted faces as they pinched their noses closed and fanned the foul fumes.

"Damn, dog, them mothafuckaz stank!" Mack said, holding his shirt over his nose and mouth.

"Babe, I think I'ma throw up," Lachaun said with watery eyes from the strong odor. Hellraiser pulled out a red bandana from his back pocket and thrashed it open. He then passed it to Lachaun for her to cover her nose and mouth. Lil' Saint, Hellraiser, and Hitt-Man weren't fazed by the overwhelming stench of the dead bodies. They'd gotten used to it over time, but the foul smell was something the others could never get used to.

Hitt-Man leaned against the side of the van, sucking on his sucker and looking at his handiwork.

"Who the fuck are these niggaz?" Hellraiser inquired about the dead goons inside of the van.

"The hittas Caleb was going to send at the rest of your crew," he reported. "I was 'pose to make that move with 'em, but I splashed them instead."

"Say, dog, close that mothafucking door," Mack said. He looked like he was about to throw up.

Hitt-Man got off the side of the van and pulled the door shut.

"I've gotta question for you, bruh," Hellraiser said to Hitt-Man.

"Spit it out," Hitt-Man replied, turning back around to him.

"Hurry back to me, baby," a grinning Lachaun told him, and she wiped the spit from the corner of her mouth.

"Not even death could keep me away from you, queen." Hellraiser smiled from behind his ski mask. Lachaun smiled hard and blushed. She then lowered her head and looked back up at him. He always knew the right things to say to her.

Hellraiser hopped out the car and shut the door quietly. He lowered his carbine at his side and pulled his hood over his head. He made his way up the street, keeping a close eye on his surroundings. His cellular vibrated with a text, and he glanced at it.

Hitt-Man: Here he comes!

Hellraiser stashed his cellphone and ran up the street.

***

Caleb rented out a three-bedroom house from a fully functioning dope addict. He knocked down its kitchen walls and two of its bedrooms. He opened the space so his workers would have enough room to cut his product. Caleb had a total of twenty naked bitchez working in what he liked to call "The Lab." All of the women rocked hair coverings, surgical masks, and latex gloves. They were cutting the heroin and sealing it in packets labeled, Killuh.

Hitt-Man and ten goons made their way around the two tables. They were armed with assault rifles and watching the workers like a hawk. Caleb was there too. He'd dropped by to see how things were going, and was satisfied with what he saw.

"Alright, I'm finna raise up outta here, big dog," Caleb told Hitt-Man and dapped him up. "Hold it down for me, loved one."

"Fa' sho'," Hitt-Man said.

Caleb dapped up the rest of the goons and said his good-byes. While he was busy doing this, Hitt-Man hoisted his assault rifle over his shoulder and shot Hellraiser a quick text. He swiftly stuck his cellular back into his pocket and walked up to the steel door. Caleb was standing at his back as he undid the locks of the door. Once Hitt-Man removed the last locks on the steel door, he said his final goodbye and bid Caleb a farewell. Once his boss had left, Hitt-Man locked the door and slid the 4 x 4 across it.

Caleb came out of the house and down the steps. He stopped at the bottom of the steps and pulled a fat ass Cuban cigar from inside of his leather coat. He clipped the end of it, stuck it between his lips, and patted himself down for a lighter. He pulled a golden Zippo lighter from out of his pocket, flipped open its lid, and produced a blue flame. He twisted the cigar from side to side as he roasted it with the flame. Sucking on the end of it, he blew smoke out of his nose and mouth then stashed the lighter inside of his pocket. Looking up into the sky, he saw the shiny full moon residing over him and listened to the crickets in the grass. He was about to walk off when he heard rustling inside of the bushes.

Caleb's forehead wrinkled as he wondered what was inside of the bushes. He pulled the cigar out of his mouth and pulled his gun from the small of his back. He cautiously approached the bushes, when a stray cat shot out of them, startling him. He was about to blast it until he realized what it was.

"Fucking cat..." Caleb cracked a grin and shook his head. He couldn't believe a goddamn cat had him on edge. Tucking his gun back at the small of his back, he went to walk away when he heard a loud, sharp whistle. His head looked over at Hellraiser, who had just pulled off his ski mask. He was wincing and holding his ribs.

"Are you okay, baby? Were you shot?" Lachaun questioned with worry dripping from her vocal cords, caressing the side of her man's face. It had always been so funny to him how his girl could go from a cold-blooded savage to a sweet, feminine, delicate flower. That was something he adored about her. She was his homie, lover, and friend.

"Nah, I didn't get hit, but I think I fractured my ribs when I dove over that fence," Hellraiser said. The left side of his ribcage was hurting like a mothafucka, and he needed some relief, bad.

"I'ma check you out once we switch cars," Lachaun told him, keeping one eye on the windshield as she affectionately pulled on his earlobe. "Did you? You know."

Hellraiser nodded his confirmation of stanking Caleb's bitch ass for laying down his baby mama. He then laid his head against Lachaun's side and placed his hand on her thigh. She kissed the top of his head and caressed the side of his face as she drove along, her full attention focused on the road ahead.

Lachaun hummed a soothing tune that eventually caused Hellraiser to shut his eyes and drift off to sleep, like a newborn baby.

Hellraiser and Lachaun disposed of their guns. They changed clothes and set their clothes and getaway car ablaze. Afterward, they hopped into the other whip that was parked at the same location. The getaway car exploded into a fireball and lit up the sky as they drove away.

"Your ribs are bruised pretty badly. We're gonna have to bandage 'em up once we get to the house," Lachaun told Hellraiser as he drove through scarcely populated streets. She was looking back and forth between Hellraiser and the windshield. She'd stopped to examine the left side of his ribs while they were in the middle of changing clothes at the explosion sight. His ribs weren't only sore to her touch, but they were discolored and purplish blue.

"We'll take care of my ribs once we get to yo' crib," Hellraiser informed her as he held his side, wincing.

***

Two nights later

The night was crisp and cold as the moon shone above the city streets. Every now and again, a car sped up Central Avenue and its wind ruffled his shirt. He was wearing a powder-blue polo, denim jeans, and Air Force Ones. He stood directly across the street from the Newton Community Police Station, scratching the inside of his arm. Although he was itchy, it wasn't because he hadn't bathed. He was a heroin addict, and he was craving his next fix.

He planned to get high after he reported a murder he'd witnessed. As bad as he wanted to now, he couldn't. The police wouldn't take him seriously if he came to give a statement while under the influence. There was no way they'd take the word of a dopefiend. This was exactly why some friends of his had made sure they cleaned him up nicely. In addition to a hot shower, they gave him a fresh haircut, a new set of clothes, and sneakers to wear down to the police station. He took a good look at himself in the mirror before he'd left and had to admit he didn't look too shabby. Based off his appearance alone, he was sure he could report what he'd seen and who he'd seen do it without drawing suspicion to himself.

The traffic light turned green and he made his way across the street. He stopped at the bottom of the stone steps

"I'm Sergeant Walton, with the Newton Division Police Department," the leading officer introduced himself and shook the manager's hand. By the way he was talking, the manager could tell he was rushing. His forehead was crinkled with curiosity as he wondered what was going on. "We have an arrest warrant for one of your tenants." He pulled out an old mug shot and showed it to him.

"This Trey—Treymaine James," the old man said, scratching his temple. "He stays up in apartment six." He looked up at unit six, which was on the second floor. "What's—what's the matter? What's going on?"

"I'll explain everything to you later, sir. Right now, I need for you to gimme the key to his place so we can do our job and arrest this guy. You got the key?"

"Sure. Lemme go get it." The old man walked away as fast as he could, keeping his eyes on the mug shot. "Lord, have mercy, what kinda shit has this boy gotten himself into?" he said to no one in particular and shook his head. He pulled his rosary out of his shirt and kissed it. He said a hushed prayer for his tenant as he entered his unit. He knew with how The Boys were planning to storm Hellraiser's unit, he'd more than likely be leaving out of there inside a body bag.

"God, watch over that young man," the old man said, heading back out of his apartment with the key to Hellraiser's unit.

***

I'll be glad when Lachaun comes back and hooks up them tacos. I'm hungry as a mothafucking hostage, Hellraiser thought as he sat up on the side of the bed and clicked the lamp light on. He then pulled a tray from under the bed and began rolling up a fat ass joint. As he prepared his joint, he looked back and forth between the show on television and the task at hand.

The television was so loud that Hellraiser didn't hear someone knocking at the door. Shortly thereafter, the front door of his apartment flew open and police officers rushed inside. Hellraiser's eyes nearly popped out their sockets when he saw the shadowy figures moving throughout his living room from the mirror hanging on his bedroom wall. The living room's lights were out, so he couldn't see that it was the police invading his home. The first thing he thought was it was some of Caleb's niggaz coming to lay him down. That was the most recent drama he'd gotten into, so he figured that was exactly who was making their move on him.

Easily, Hellraiser sat the joint down on his bed and took his gun from underneath his pillow. His face scrunched up heatedly as he chambered a round into it.

These fucking cockroaches done ran up into my shit, thinking I'ma be an easy one. On the dead homies, y'all got me fucked up, Hellraiser thought as he gritted his teeth and pounced up from his bed, lifting his blower. At this time, his cellphone vibrated and rang from where it was lying on the nightstand.

"You mothafuckaz done broke into the Devil's lair, allow me to welcome you to Hell properly!" Hellraiser barked viciously, with spit flying from off his big lips. As soon as he saw a flicker of movement in the darkness, he started blasting.

Bocka, bocka, bocka!

"Aaaaahhh!"

Hellraiser heard one of the shadowy figures holler in agony. He continued to fire, and he heard another one of the figures howl in pain, collapsing to the floor. The next thing

Hellraiser saw was fire flickering in the darkness of the living room. He gritted as fire ripped through his shoulder and propelled him back against the wall. His slamming up against the wall left the mirror hanging sideways. He fell to the floor but quickly scrambled to his feet. Using the bed for cover, he squeezed off at the shadowy figures as they moved in on him.

Bocka, bocka, bocka!

"If I'm going out, I'm taking you bitchez with me!" Hellraiser called out and continued to fire rapidly.

Bocka, bocka, bocka!

Swiftly, Hellraiser smacked the lamp from off the dresser and it broke, extinguishing its light. He put a bullet in the television screen and turned out its light, leaving his bedroom in darkness. Now his enemies couldn't see him, but he knew which way they were coming, so the odds of survival tilted somewhat in his favor. The intruders, the police, couldn't see his face, but he was smiling from where he was hidden behind the bed, loading up another magazine into his Glock.

"Put your gun down and—" one of the police officers began, but he was cut short.

"Fuck y'all niggaz! This Bloods!" Hellraiser roared and started blazing at their asses again.

Bocka, bocka, bocka, bocka!

Meanwhile, Lachaun stood behind Hellraiser's apartment listening to the gunfire and seeing the muzzle flashes in the window.

"Nooo, nooooooo!" a teary-eyed Lachaun screamed and screamed, fearing her fiancé had been executed. Cellphone in hand, she ran up the stairs to the top floor as fast as she could. She was trying to come to her man's aid before it was too late.

***

Hellraiser slowly stirred awake, peeling his eyes open and wincing in pain. The morphine he'd been given was beginning to wear off, and he could feel the three bullets he'd taken to the torso. His mouth was so dry that he couldn't swallow, and his vision was blurry. He felt a fly land on his cheek and crawl toward his forehead. He went to swat it, but something snagged his wrist and caused a *ting* to resonate inside the room. Hellraiser frowned when he looked at his wrist and saw a metal bracelet locked around it. He looked to the door of his room and saw a cop sitting down reading a newspaper. Right then, the memories that led to him being shot and held captive inside of the hospital flooded his mind.

"Aw, shiiit," Hellraiser said in a hushed tone. He let his head drop back against his pillow and closed his eyes. He already knew where he was going from here—the mothafucking pen!

***

A lot of cash exchanged hands, a lot of promises were made, and a lot of favors were done, and fortunately for Hellraiser, his attorney was able to get him a fifteen-year sentence. It was a long stretch, but it beat the life sentence he was looking at for Caleb's murder and busting at One Time. Hellraiser knew it would be a long time before he saw the light of day, but that didn't stop the responsibilities he had as a man. He still had to take care of his family. So, it wasn't to anyone's surprise that he played enforcer to his father, OG, who was serving life behind bars. OG was an old head that

133

had been putting it down for the set since Hellraiser was a little snotty nose baby, running around in shitty pampers. His hustle was heroin, and it provided him a life of luxury behind the walls. Hellraiser often joked that OG should have his own television show called: *The Lifestyles of the Rich and Incarcerated.*

Anyway, the old head's lead enforcer got sent to death row on the account of a murder beef he'd caught on his behalf. So he needed some muscle to back him when it came time to collect and niggaz weren't trying to cough up that dough. That's where Hellraiser came in. His job was to make an example out of mothafuckaz that played with his father's money. Most of them un-assed the cash once they got a beatdown, but there were some that met with the deadly end of Hellraiser's shank when they didn't come up with their debt. That's how Hellraiser was able to make his money. Nearly every dollar he made under his father, he sent it back home to Lachaun to make sure his family was taken care of.

In between keeping his foot on the necks of the mark-ass niggaz indebted to OG, Hellraiser spent the rest of his time chopping it up with Lachaun and checking in on his son. He'd used some of the gwap he made as his father's hired hand to buy himself a cellphone. This way, he didn't have to use the jacks in the prison they were charging convicts an arm and a leg to use. When he wasn't checking up on his loved ones, he was working out with the other bloods in his car and kicking the shit about prison politics. He had a program that he stuck to religiously. Time seemed to fly by with him keeping himself busy, but still, prison was prison. And no nigga in his right mind wanted to be there. There wasn't anything like freedom.

***

2010
Ten years later

Hellraiser was missing his loved ones like crazy, especially his son, KiMani. He'd heard he was following in his footsteps. He'd signed up with the same gang and had took to calling himself, Lil' Hell. He'd gotten word that he and another little homeboy by the name of Arnez were terrorizing the streets and getting into everything there was to get into. Hellraiser's mother was an old woman, and she couldn't do anything with KiMani. He did whatever the fuck he wanted to do, and she couldn't tell him anything. Lachaun chopped it up with him, but her intervention didn't seem to work either.

Hellraiser thought that he'd have a better time trying to reason with the kid, but everything he said went into one ear and out of the other. When they did talk, it seemed like all he wanted to do was talk about street shit. What bitchez he was fucking, how much money he was getting, who he'd gotten into it with, and who were the ghetto stars in the hood. Nothing else seemed to matter to the young nigga. That's when he realized he'd lost him, and the streets had him. The thought of his son ending up behind bars like him, continuing the cycle, fucked him up. But there wasn't anything he could do about it as long as he was locked up.

The past ten years had been quite kind to Hellraiser where his physical features were concerned. He didn't look like he'd aged at all. In fact, the only way you could really tell that he had aged was due to his salt and pepper goatee. Well, that and the sprinkles of gray throughout his hair. He felt that he'd gotten too old to sport cornrows, so he cut them off and settled on a fade as a hairstyle. As of now, it was lights out and he was laid out on his bottom bunk, with his contraband cellphone glued to his ear. His eyes were closed as he talked to Lachaun, visualizing how she'd look in front of him holding this conversation.

"Why are you so quiet right now, baby? What chu doing over there?" Hellraiser asked.

"Ooh, nothing, just looking at my wedding ring," Lachaun replied happily. He could hear the excitement in her voice. They'd gotten married nine years ago, but agreed to have an official ceremony once he was released from prison.

"Oh, yeah? That's why you're smiling?"

"Wait a minute, how do you know I'm smiling?"

"'Cause, I broke out, and now I'm inside yo' closet, watching you."

"Yeah, right, nigga, yo' ass still in there. I'm not stupid."

"You sure? 'Cause I just heard yo' black ass open the closet door."

They laughed their asses off.

"Nah, but for real though, baby, how'd you know I was smiling?"

"I could hear the saliva in yo' mouth and feel your aura through the phone. Crazy, right?"

"Yeah, that is something—I can't wait to see you next week."

"I can't wait to see you either, ma, for real, for real."

"Oh, my god, I can't believe we're gonna be someone's parents."

"I know, right? Shit's wild."

There was a long silence between them before Lachaun broke it.

"I love you, Trey. I love you so, so much," Lachaun told him, her voice cracking emotionally. She sniffled, and he could tell she was wiping the tears from her eyes. "I can't wait for you to come home so we can be together. Promise me, promise me you're gonna make it home and we're gonna be together forever and ever," she said, her voice cracking the more she talked. She was full-on crying now. Hearing her in such distress made Hellraiser sit up, holding his contraband cellphone to his ear, forehead wrinkled with genuine concern.

"Hey, hey, hey, ma, what's wrong? What the matter?" Hellraiser asked with worry in his voice. He glanced at the door to make sure there weren't any corrections officers watching him.

Hellraiser listened as she took the time to wipe her dripping eyes and blow her nose. She cleared her throat before she started back talking again.

"I'm—I'm sorry, babe, I don't mean—I don't mean to put any pressure on you," she assured him. "Let's just change the subject."

"Nah, unh, unh." He shook his head, leaned forward, and allowed his free hand to dangle between his legs. "No, baby, I'm not finna let chu do that. If you don't get what's bothering you off your chest, it's gonna stay on your mind. I'm your husband, and I hold nothing above you. I'm here for you. Talk to me, now."

There was silence. She took a deep breath before starting back up again.

"I'm just worried, baby."

"Worried about what?" He sat up and listened closely.

"Look at where you're at? I mean, what if something happens to you before you get out and you don't make it home? What if one day I get a call that you're—that you're—"

"Shhhhh, unh, unh," he hushed her, shutting his eyes briefly and shaking his head. "Don't talk like that. You say

thugged it out these ten years he'd been on lock. He knew for a fact he wouldn't have been able to make it without the love of his family.

"I love you, ma," Hellraiser said softly.

"I love you too, baby," Lachaun responded groggily, taking him by surprise. He grinned and listened to her sleeping a few minutes longer before disconnecting the call. He stashed his contraband cellphone in its hiding place and shut his eyes for a good night's sleep.

***

Two months later

Hellraiser lay in bed asleep with his cellphone in his hand. He'd accidentally drifted off while talking to Lachaun. Suddenly, the cellular's display lit up, and it vibrated in his fist. His eyelids and nose twitched, feeling the shaking of the device in his grasp. Realizing it was the vibration of the cell traveling up his arm, he looked at its screen. It was Lachaun. He figured she was hitting him back like she always did when they'd fallen asleep on the phone together. His cell phone only had one bar left. So he was going to tell her he'd call her back once he let his phone charge. Sitting up on his bunk, he answered the call and placed his cellular to his ear.

Eyes shut, massaging the bridge of his nose, he said, groggily, "Aye, babe, I got, like, one bar left, so lemme char—" He looked up with a furrowed brow, hearing Lachaun whimpering and sniffling. His heart sank, and his stomach twisted in knots. He wondered if something had happened to the baby, or if the streets had caught up with KiMani, and he was dead. He feared the worst when she finally told him what was up. "Babe, what's wrong? What's the matter? What's going on?" He was now on his feet, pacing the floor of his six-by-nine cell, heart racing. The anticipation of the bad news was driving him crazy, but he tried his best to remain calm. "Lachaun, is something wrong with the baby? Did something happen to KiMani?"

"The baby and KiMani are fine, baby," she told him, sniffling again.

He ran his hand down his face and sighed with relief. He then placed his hand under his arm and leaned against the wall, staring up at the ceiling. "Well, what's up? Why are you crying, ma?"

"It's—it's your mother, baby. KiMani found her—he found her in bed—dead." The moment she told him his mother was dead, she broke down sobbing loudly.

"Oh, no, no, no, no," Hellraiser said aloud, turning to the wall he'd been leaning against. Tears streamed down his face as he pounded his fist against the wall. More and more tears streamed down his face, and a snot bubble expanded out of his left nostril. It popped and slid down over his top lip. "Ooooh, God, why? Whyyyyy?" he screamed and pounded the wall harder. He then threw his cell phone at the wall. It deflected off of it and flew across the cramped cell. Seeing through a haze of red, his nostrils flared, and he clenched his jaws. He balled his fists tight and started kicking the wall.

"Yo, I think them niggaz up in there fighting!" he heard one of the convicts to the left of his cell say.

"Oh, shit! Who getting they ass whipped?" he heard another convict say from the right of his cell. Right after, there was heaving pounding at the doors of all of the cells on the tier Hellraiser was on. All of the convicts were screaming out profanities and egging on what they thought was a fight.

Meanwhile, Hellraiser went crazy. He snatched pictures of his family, magazine clippings, and centerfolds of video vixens from his wall. He then smacked off everything occupying his desktop, and sent it flying across his cell.

"Blood, what's going on? What happened?" OG asked, worried, climbing down from the top bunk. He was a sixty-something-year-old man who stood a tad over six feet. He had a copper complexion and a slender physique. He had a thick salt and pepper goatee, and a receding hairline that led to a small, unkempt afro. The old head was one of the original gangstas from Hellraiser's hood. He came from an era where fist fights were the norm when it came to combating the enemies of one's neighborhood. If it wasn't fist fights, then it was a knife, a baseball bat, a pipe, or whatever object a nigga could get his hands on to do some real bodily damage.

It wasn't until the eighties when guns came into play, and when they did, OG got real acquainted with them. He garnered himself a fierce reputation warring with his opps. Unfortunately for him, his past came back to haunt him and he winded up with a lifelong stretch. When he went in, he was OG Henry James. But Henry James was eventually dropped from his moniker, when the younger heads started referring to him as OG, since he was one of the eldest G's in their car.

A startled Hellraiser whipped around to OG with glassy, pink eyes accumulating tears. He'd forgotten he had a cellmate when he'd been given the horrible news about his mother's passing. So, hearing someone behind him had taken him off guard. Although he never wanted anyone to see him so vulnerable, he figured his old man would understand the way he was feeling then. He'd lost his mother, and it was killing him. He was dying inside.

For a while, Hellraiser didn't say anything, he just stood there staring at OG, with a trembling bottom lip. More and more water collected in his eyes until tears jetted down his cheeks unevenly.

"M—mom's—she's—she's dead, Pops. My—my old bird's gone," he told him, and bowed his head, teardrops falling from his eyes rapidly. His shoulders rocked back and forth as he cried, teardrops splashing on the cool cement floor.

OG picked up the broken pieces of Hellraiser's cellular and flushed them down the toilet. He then gave him a fatherly hug.

The bad news felt like a sniper's bullet through the heart. Ruby was the love of OG's life. Although they'd been separated for quite some time, they were still legally married. She wrote him consistently and visited every chance she'd gotten. He was still very much in love with her, so he wanted to break down like his son had. The only thing that stopped him was the need of being a pillar of strength for him. He had to remain strong for his boy's sake. He understood more than ever, he needed him now, and nothing was going to stop him from being there for him.

"It's gonna be alright, son," OG consoled him, hugging him tighter. He knew what he was going through losing his mother. He'd lost his mother, sister, and countless homeboys while he was holed up in the pen. It was hell. And some days, he didn't think he would survive. He held everything in and acted like he wasn't fazed, but his grief was killing him inside. He knew how important it was for a man to have an outlet. You know, someone to confide in and talk about his feelings with? Well, he was going to be that person for his son—Hellraiser. He felt like he owed that to him, since he couldn't be there for him growing up and he was his father. "I've been there, kid. I've been exactly where you are, but I tell you what—we're gonna get through this—I promise. I promise you."

OG held Hellraiser as he cried. They could hear the parade of stampeding, booted feet heading down the tier to them, but they ignored it. They knew it was the corrections officers coming to their cell. There was the jingling of keys outside the door, and then the door was pulled open. The COs rushed inside with canisters of mace, wearing protective shields over their faces, with billy clubs at the ready.

When OG looked up and saw the corrections officers at his door ready to ride out, he held up his hand and talked to the commanding officer, who he had a good relationship with. "It's okay, it's okay—I got it, Minks. My boy's just dealing witta lot, is all."

CO Minks, who was a burly white man with graying hair, nodded understandingly. He gave the signal for his men to fall back, and they did as he ordered them. Everyone lowered their mace and billy clubs and then left out of the cell, leaving the two men alone.

Hellraiser sobbed long and hard against OG. The old head continued to console him, hugging him even tighter and rocking him back and forth.

"Everything is gonna be alright. I got cha. I got cha," OG assured him with a calm tone, handling him like a father should.

Chapter Ten
A few days later

Hellraiser stood over the sink before the metal reflector, brushing his teeth. Occasionally, he'd walk over to the toilet and spit in it. This was common prison etiquette when you had a cell mate. While Hellraiser was occupied with taking care of his hygiene, OG was busy playing solitaire.

"Yeah, that mothafucka Dabo has been sitting on that scratch he owes me for a minute now. Son of a bitch been ducking and dodging for the longest." OG shook his head as he complained. His attention was focused on the cards laid out before him. "Dumbass thinks he can avoid his debt in the joint. Shiiiiit, you can't hide from no nigga up in here. I ain't killed me a nigga in twenty-three years, but his young ass gon' make me come outta retirement." He stopped playing with the cards and looked at Hellraiser. "See, that lil' bitch doesn't think fat meat is greasy, but I'ma show 'em otherwise. You feel me?" he asked, but didn't wait for a response. He went back to playing solitaire.

Hellraiser finished brushing his teeth, wiped his mouth, and dried his hands. He then approached his father's bunk and tapped his leg for his attention.

"Pops, I'm not about to let chu get cho hands dirty. That's what chu got me for," Hellraiser told him. "I'm yo' soldier, so fall back. You don't gotta worry about nothing. I'ma handle this busta-ass nigga for you, and make sure you get paid."

"Aww, son, I don't wanna burden you with business," OG told him. "You're going to your mother's funeral. You shouldn't be doing anything but giving yourself time to grieve."

"I feel you, Pops. But this is business." Hellraiser jabbed

his finger down into the thin mattress. "Business doesn't stop for anyone, so it has to be taken care of. Okay?" he asked, holding out his fist.

OG grinned and nodded, dapping him up.

Hellraiser finished getting ready for the funeral and looked himself over. He turned to his father, who was standing on the side of him.

"How I look, old man?" Hellraiser inquired.

"Like you gotta court date." OG smiled and adjusted his tie.

Hellraiser laughed. "You're a regular comedian today. You know that, old man? I should kick yo' ass." He backed up and threw playful punches at him. OG bobbed, weaved, and threw some of his own punches at him. They had a good laugh and then they became serious.

"I love you, son," OG told Hellraiser, and they embraced.

"I love you too, Pops."

Tears slowly slid down OG's cheeks unevenly as he held his son. "Do me a favor and say goodbye to your mother for me. Tell her I appreciate her for taking care of you while I was in this shit hole. And tell her—tell her I've never stopped loving her. She's still my soulmate—the only one for me."

OG broke their embrace and swiped away his tears with his curled finger.

"I will, Pops. I promise I will," Hellraiser assured him as he gripped his shoulder comfortingly. "You gonna be okay?"

OG nodded as he sniffled and took a deep breath. He managed a weak smile as he looked into Hellraiser's eyes. "Yeah, son, I'm okay. Look, you better gone and get outta here. You don't wanna be late now."

"Okay," Hellraiser said and gave him another hug. They

held each other for a long while before breaking their embrace. Hellraiser patted his old man on his shoulder and made his way out of the cell.

***

A big white van with gates covering all of its windows from the inside, save for the windshield, drove up the cemetery's road. It sped past several tombstones, headstones, and mausoleums before it pulled up to the funeral home. The van parked up on the grassy hill, which was flooded with whips, some old, some new. The driver of the hulking vehicle, who was an African-American guard, killed its engine and hopped out, making his way to the rear of it. He was accompanied by a Hispanic guard who'd been riding shotgun with him. Both men were dressed in similar attire. They wore caps, windbreakers with 'Sheriff' on the back of them, a Kevlar bulletproof vest underneath their tan uniform shirt, and a belt containing their holstered gun and mace, among other items.

The African-American guard unlocked the double doors of the van and pulled them open. He stood aside as his partner, the Hispanic guard, helped Hellraiser out of the back of the van. Hellraiser was fitted in a skinny, midnight-blue tie, soft gray suit that hugged his muscular arms and legs, and leather midnight-blue dress shoes. He was in full restraints with his wrists, waist, and ankles shackled. When the guard shut the door, he and his partner grabbed Hellraiser under an arm each and escorted him to the funeral home. The silver chains of his shackles made their own jingle as he shuffled along, trying his best to keep up with his chaperones.

The sky suddenly darkened and thunder grumbled like

147

the belly of a hungry giant. Lightning flashed from above and small raindrops hurled downward, pitter patting against Hellraiser's shoulder, darkening his soft gray suit. Narrowing his eyes and squinting his face, he looked up into the clouds, watching the rain splatter against his face. As soon as the water hit him, it ran down his forehead and cheeks, dripping off his chin. He brought his head back down as tears slid down his face, mixing with the rain water crashing against his face. He was thankful it had rained that day, because it would help to hide his grieving. He didn't want anyone inside of the funeral home to see him vulnerable. He was a gangsta, and his reputation meant everything to him. It was all he had to help him survive behind the walls, besides his family.

I remember you used to always say that when it rained it was the angels in heaven crying for all the hell we were going through down here. I believe you, Momma, I really do. I know it's you up there crying out for me and everyone else that lost someone today, Hellraiser thought of his mother as he was escorted towards the opened doors of the funeral home, seeing the backs of men, women, and children wearing their best suits and dresses for the sad occasion.

The closer Hellraiser got towards the doors of the funeral home, the clearer he could hear the powerful and commanding voice of the minister giving a speech.

"We are here today to pay our tribute and our respect to a woman of God, our sister, Ruby Robertson. Not only have people from this congregation and community gathered, but many ministers have come—ministers who have respected Ruby as a friend, and have loved her as family. To know Ruby Robertson James was to love her...."

Hellraiser made his way up the cement steps, drawing the attention of those that had packed out the funeral home.

He saw a lot of his family in attendance, which he wasn't surprised by. His uncles, aunts and cousins, nieces and nephews greeted him smirks and nods of acknowledgement. He returned their gestures with a grin and nod. The further he drew inside of the tenement, the more attention he commandeered. He got nods and waves from friends of his mother and members of her church, some of whom were dealing with declining health themselves. Some of them had a walker, a cane, or were sitting in wheelchairs, with oxygen tanks attached to the back of them. They also had see-through oxygen masks over their noses and mouths to help them breathe.

Hellraiser remembered them all. They never did have anything nice to say about him, so fuck them! On several occasions that he'd escorted his mother to church, he'd walked up on them talking about him. Once, they said he was the spawn of Satan and would eventually be the death of his mother. The same folks talking shit about him would be right back in his face, showing all thirty-twos and telling him they loved the bond he and his mother had—and how he took care of her and what not.

Fake-ass holy rollers, y'all can kiss my gangsta ass. Jokes on y'all, I didn't kill my momma. She died peacefully in her sleep of natural causes, Hellraiser thought as the guards found a place for them to stand. They took up space at the back of the room where they could see everyone present—as well as everyone coming and going.

"...We would be less than honest if we said that our hearts have not ached over this situation. We are not too proud to acknowledge that we have come here today trusting that God would minister to our hearts, and give us strength as we continue in our walk with Him..." the minister continued on with his speech. Hellraiser glanced in his

149

direction and found him standing behind the podium. He was a tall, heavyset man with a shiny, bald head and a thin salt and pepper mustache. The meat of his neck hung over the collar of his button-up dress shirt, which was underneath a black and purple clergy robe with crosses on either side of it. He occasionally looked down on the flat surface of the podium at his spiel as he delivered his speech. Every so often, he'd swallow the spit in his throat and wipe the beads of sweat from his forehead with his folded handkerchief.

A smile stretched across Hellraiser's face when he saw his old crew standing across the room from him: Mack, Lil' Saint, Julian, and Lachaun. The homies were all dressed to the nines, wearing feathered brims and a vest underneath their suits. Hellraiser thought they looked like a couple of old school gangstas off of the *Hoodlum* movie set. Although they all weren't active in the gang life anymore, they were still flying their colors like they were, as far as the color of their attire was concerned. Even Lachaun was looking her best in her formfitting red dress, which showcased her oval-shaped pregnant belly. She'd dropped the traditional corn-rows she usually wore and now sported her hair in long, bouncy curls. Her angelic face was beat to perfection, and she was glowing—glowing like she'd been cast down from the beautiful, cloudy skies of heaven.

Lachaun, whose forehead was shiny with sweat, was fanning herself with Ruby's obituary while engaged in a hushed conversation with the rest of the fellas. Hellraiser figured she must have felt his eyes on her, because she looked in his direction. She couldn't stop smiling once she saw his face. And neither could he. It was taking all he had not to break away from those guards and run over to her. He desperately wanted to kiss her, hug her, and rub her belly. Instead, he opted to wave at her. She waved and blew him a kiss.

Mack, Lil' Saint, and Julian looked in the direction she'd blown a kiss and saw Hellraiser. They broke out in smiles and threw their heads back like, *What up, nigga?* Mack and Julian threw up their hood and Hellraiser returned the gesture. They were all happy to see him, and planned to holler at him once the ceremony had come to a close.

Although they were pushing fifty, the homies looked good for their ages. They showed little signs of graying and appeared to work out regularly. They all wrote him often and came to visit whenever they'd gotten a chance to. Mack had taken his share from the Rude Bwois hit along with some paper he had stashed and opened up his own gentlemen's club. He named it Mack Daddy. He had the bitchez he was pimping on The Blade provide the entertainment. The place was a hit! It stayed packed, even on Mondays. Strip clubs hardly got business on a Monday. You could dance, drink, smoke, do drugs, and if your money was right, you could get yourself a little backroom action, you know—pussy and/or head.

Julian wasn't doing too badly for himself either. He'd taken his cut from the lick and bought Old Man Griffith's place—Bottoms Up. His establishment was a landmark in the hood. On any day of the week, you could catch anybody that was somebody shooting the breeze with him over a cold one. Bottoms Up was like a fraternity house. The patrons there were like family. The bar was indisputably the Cheers of the urban community.

Although the homies always talked about how they were going to leave the streets alone and go legit, Hellraiser doubted them—and rightfully so. They were all waist deep in the game and didn't show any signs of slowing down—ever. Seeing the homies had made good on their claims,

151

made Hellraiser proud of them. As proud of them as he was, it was Lil' Saint's one-hundred-eighty degree turnaround that wowed him the most. The homie appeared to have gone through a complete transformation. He'd gone from a cold-blooded killa to the minister of one of the biggest churches in Southern California. He'd even gotten married and had a couple of kids. He owned several rental properties, a mansion in Beverly Hills, a Bentley Continental, a Maybach, and a yacht. Lil' Saint was doing damn well for himself, and Hellraiser couldn't be happier for him.

Hellraiser scanned the funeral home's pews looking for KiMani, but he didn't see him at all. He looked back to Lachaun and asked her where he was through the movement of his mouth. She shrugged and mouthed to him that "she didn't know." She then asked the rest of the crew where he was. They shook their heads and said they didn't know. Well, that's what Hellraiser gathered by their body language and lip movements.

Hellraiser bowed his head and took a deep breath. He was looking forward to seeing his boy that day. Although he'd talked to him a couple of times over the phone, he hadn't seen him in a while. Hellraiser looked up in the minister's direction when he heard him say this:

"...At this time, we will permit Ruby's loved ones to say their final goodbyes to her before she returns home to the Lord's kingdom..." The minister then cleared his throat with his fist to his mouth and wiped the sweat from his forehead once again. He stepped down from the podium and one of the pallbearers stepped forth, wearing white cloth gloves, unlocking Ruby's coffin and lifting its lid. He then stepped aside and held his wrist at his waist. Another pallbearer directed the audience on the right side to form a line in the aisle. He then motioned for them to come forward to view

Ruby's body, stepping aside so they'd have a clear path to her.

"We'll go up once everyone's gon' up," the African-American guard told Hellraiser in his ear in a hushed tone, to which he nodded understandingly.

Hellraiser stood by watching as the audiences on both sides of the funeral went up to pay their final respects to his mother. Once they'd all gone up, the guards escorted him to the aisle where they flanked him toward his mother's coffin. Her coffin was pearly white with shiny brass handles. It was surrounded by beautiful floral arrangements of all colors and sizes. His mother, who was now thirty pounds heavier than she was the last time he'd seen her, was holding a dozen rich yellow, black-eyed daisies at her torso. Her thick silver hair was styled in long locs that Lachaun had come down to the home to do herself. She'd also done a wonderful job with her makeup. She was wearing a sheer-white evening gown and a crown of vines with yellow flowers decorating them. Sitting off to the side were portraits of all sizes, representing the past and present of Ruby's life.

As Hellraiser made his way down the aisle, he could feel the hot sting of tears in his eyes. Right after, his eyes turned pink and began to water. A lump of hurt the size of a golf ball formed in his throat, but he managed to swallow it. He blinked away the wetness in his eyes and loosened the tie around his neck. Seeing the homies and his wife made him forget where he was, but he was quickly reminded when reality smacked him across the face. Today was his mother's funeral. This would be the last time he'd see her, and he could literally feel his heart crumbling into pieces. With that came the overwhelming grief that seemed to pour down his face in big buckets, slicking his cheeks wet.

Hellraiser lifted his curled finger to his eyes and swiped

away the teardrops that threatened to fall from them. He felt his knees buckle the closer he got to his mother's coffin, but he recovered his equilibrium and held fast. He snorted back the snot that attempted to fall from his nose, held his head high, and stuck out his chest. When he reached Ruby's coffin, he admired his mother's beauty. She'd always been a looker, and she never had a problem getting a man. She had caramel skin, hazel-green eyes, full lips, and the most stunning smile anyone had ever seen.

"Heyyy, Momma, you look so beautiful today," Hellraiser greeted her with a one-sided smile, caressing her stiff hand. "They really did a good job with you. You look so peaceful. If I didn't know any better, I would have thought you were asleep." His eyes quickly gathered tears, and he could feel them about to slide down his cheeks. He squeezed his eyes shut to hold them back and snorted back snot again. He then peeled his eyes back open and looked back down at his mother, caressing her hand again. "I'm gonna miss you, Ma. Make sure you save me a seat up there. Watch out for all of us down here. I love you. See you when I get there, queen." He caressed the side of her face with his shackled hand and leaned down into the coffin. In a hushed tone, he told her everything his father told him to tell her. Afterward, he kissed her lovingly on her cheek and stood upright. He took one last look at his mother, bid her a farewell, and allowed the guards to lead him away.

For as long as Hellraiser could remember, his mother had his back. All the hell he raised coming up, he was surprised that she never turned her back on him. In her eyes, he couldn't do any wrong, no matter his faults. She went to every single one of his court dates when he'd gotten locked up for an unlicensed firearm. She was sure to put money on his books, and she visited him faithfully.

Hellraiser knew he would eventually run his mother down into an early grave if he kept getting into trouble. Every time he winded up behind bars, he swore to her he was going to change once he got out. And every time, he turned out to be a liar. It wasn't that he was lying to her purposefully. He actually meant what he said, but the call of the streets was too loud for him to ignore. It was like he was addicted to them. He was a fiend and it was his drug.

He reasoned that he couldn't help that the life of a street nigga was in his blood. His daddy before him, OG, was a street nigga, and his father before him was one also. His grandfather used to run numbers and sell bootleg liquor. The little country boy from Little Rock, Arkansas wouldn't know an honest day of work if he bumped into it. He got it out of the mud to take care of his family.

The Hispanic guard glanced at his black digital watch and looked at his partner. "Aye, we've gotta be getting back."

"Alright," the African-American guard said, pulling Hellraiser along.

Damn, I'm not gon' getta chance to holler at Lachaun and nem, Hellraiser thought, looking over his shoulder at his crew. They all wore frowns as they looked at him like, *What's going on?* He shrugged. Lachaun held up his mother's obituary and mouthed to him that she was going to mail it to him. The rest of the fellas tapped their fists against their chests, letting him know to stay solid and that they had love for him.

***

A blood-red 1978 Chevrolet Impala with a mesh chrome grille and matching Dayton rims and fourteen-inch tires pulled up outside of the funeral home. Its sideview mirrors and trunk rattled from the sound system pumping 2Pac Shakur's "So Many Tears." The driver of the ghetto classic whip threw it in park and murdered its engine. Then, allowed the music to play.

Back in elementary, I thrived on misery
Left me alone I grew up amongst a dying breed
Inside my mind couldn't find a place to rest
Until I got that Thug Life tatted on my chest

There was so much smoke inside of the confines of the Impala that it looked like the buildings' crash site on 9/11. The driver, Arnez, was laid back in the seat. He had hooded, glassy, pink eyes and a fat ass blunt hanging from his full lips, stuffed with Killa Cali's finest. Arnez was a sixteen-year-old dude with an almond hue, with abstract designs cut into his low-cut fade. He wore a white applejack and a red Coogi sweater. A platinum and diamond tennis necklace with a diamond-studded cross hung around his neck.

A fourteen-year-old KiMani was lying back in his seat as well. He was even drunker and higher than Arnez. His hair was styled in cornrows, just like his father before he was incarcerated. In fact, the youngsta looked even more like him now that he'd gotten older. He was draped in a red Adidas sweatsuit whose hood he wore over his head. Hanging out of the collar of his hoodie was a gold necklace, which held onto a round pendant surrounded by diamonds. The picture inside of the pendant had been taken long ago; sometime in the 1950s. It was of a young Ruby Robertson James rocking a big ass afro, mustard-yellow turtleneck, and denim overalls.

KiMani's hand was wrapped around a big gold bottle of Louis Roederer's Cristal. He stared at the windshield of the Chevrolet, watching the rain pitter patter against it. The raindrops created their own music as they thumped against the glass and slid downward. KiMani couldn't help thinking how much those raindrops reminded him of teardrops—his teardrops—the very teardrops that were dripping from his pink eyes now.

KiMani had lost his grandmother, who he affectionately referred to as Big Ma. She had been the closest woman he had to a mother besides Lachaun. Sure, he had Shaniqua once upon a time, but that bitch was the human form of Satan to him. You couldn't convince him otherwise the way she'd verbally and physically abused him. Big Ma was who he believed his mother truly was. She was everything he wanted in a mother—and then some. She showed him the love that he'd never gotten from his biological mother. You would have thought she'd been the one that had pushed him out of her womb.

Losing Big Ma had him fucked up mentally. His birth mother was a fucking psychopath and he'd lost his father to the prison system. Often, he wondered was his life a mistake given the fact that nearly everyone he loved had been taken away from him. He thought about committing suicide since the passing of his grandmother. He tried to hang himself in the garage with a length of rope he'd found, but the bar that operated the garage door broke. It left him with a nasty burn around his neck and a knot on the side of his head the size of a grapefruit. When he finally regained consciousness, he took the botched suicide attempt as a sign for him to keep on going—to keep on living—and that's exactly what he was going to do. Besides, his hood had plenty of opps that needed to be smoked, and he wasn't about to let his death have them bitch-ass niggaz sighing with relief.

Arnez looked at KiMani's drenched face and couldn't help feeling sad for him. He grew up without his parents. So he'd never know the pain that came with losing them. He knew it was impossible to miss something he'd never had. Arnez was an orphan. His mother was a high school dropout turned dope fiend. She'd given birth to him and left him inside of a trash bin, in an alley, in the back of a Chinese takeout restaurant. The garbage man had dumped the bin inside the back of his truck along with other trash. The garbage cushioned baby Arnez's fall, but it was his wailing that saved him from being crushed by the trash compactor. The garbage man dropped him off at a hospital that put him in the system. When he came of age, he ran into the waiting arms of the streets and she nurtured him like a loving mother. She fed him, clothed him, and provided him with room and board. And for that, he had unconditional love for her—he could never turn his back on her—ever.

When Arnez and KiMani linked up, it was like they'd known each other all of their lives. Since they'd met, they'd been with each other every day. When they weren't fucking with the local hood rats, or smoking, drinking, and getting high, they were hustling—getting money. Arnez had taken KiMani under his wing and showed him the ropes. In him, KiMani found his mentor. In KiMani, Arnez found what he always wanted in life—family.

Arnez turned the volume on his stereo down, took the blunt out of his mouth, and gripped KiMani's shoulder brotherly. "You straight, Kid?"

"Nah, Blood, I'm fucked up." KiMani looked at him, swiping the tears from his eyes swiftly. "I'm reallll fucked up," he admitted, keeping it one hundred. He hadn't spent a day sober since he discovered Big Ma's dead body. It seemed like getting drunk and high was the only thing that eased his emotional torment. Even then, he found it hard to say his final goodbyes to her. He wasn't sure how he'd react to seeing her lying in that coffin. Truthfully, he was just going to say fuck it and not even show up to her funeral. He most definitely would have been a no-show if Arnez hadn't convinced him to do otherwise.

"Me too, dog, Big Ma had always been good to me. She treated me like family," Arnez told him. "This one hurt—this one hurt us to the cores of our souls, but chu know what? You and I are gonna soldier up and make it through this. You and me, loved one." He switched hands with the wafting blunt and gave KiMani a gangsta hug. "I love you, my nigga."

"I love you too, nigga," KiMani replied before taking the gold champagne bottle to the head, guzzling it. He spilled some of it down his chin and wiped it off with the back of his hand.

Arnez took a couple more pulls from the end of his blunt and blew another cloud of smoke out. He mashed out what was left of the bleezy inside of the ashtray.

"Come on, my nigga, let's get up in here so we can pay our respects to our girl," Arnez told him.

"Alright," KiMani said, taking another drink of champagne and then putting its top back in. He sat the bottle down on the floor between his legs and hopped out, slamming the door behind him.

Chapter Eleven

KiMani and Arnez came together after hopping out of the old school whip. Arnez glanced behind him and locked the doors of his ride with the small black, square remote on his key-ring, and the car beeped. Arnez stuffed the keys in his pocket and threw his arm around KiMani's neck, pulling him closer. Together, they made hurried footsteps towards the opened double doors of the funeral home. They frowned up as the rain pelted their clothing and faces, slicking them wet. They'd gotten halfway to the cement steps of the sacred tenement when Hellraiser emerged flanked by two guards. The African-American guard was in the middle of opening the umbrella to combat the rain shower while the Hispanic one stuck by his charge's side.

Hellraiser frowned as the raindrops pelted his face and suit. Water ran down his face and dripped off his chin as he stared at the two men approaching him. By this time, the African-American guard had opened the umbrella and held it over their heads and was escorting him to the van. The closer Hellraiser got to the two men, the more their features became clearer to him.

"KiMani? KiMani, is that you? Is that you, son?" Hellraiser asked excitedly. His eyes lit up and his mouth hung open.

Suddenly, KiMani and Arnez stopped walking. They stood in the middle of the cemetery road with the rain beating down upon them.

"Pops!" KiMani said, just as excited as his father. Arnez's forehead wrinkled as he looked back and forth between father and son. The next thing he knew, KiMani took off running toward his father. He tripped and fell onto the spongy, grassy lawn of the cemetery but quickly scrambled back up on his shell-toe sneakers. He continued his sprint towards his old man, ignoring the muddy wetness on the knees of his Adidas sweatpants.

The Hispanic sheriff's officer, Officer Hernandez, went to stop KiMani from engaging his father, but Officer Allen, the African American, held up his hand for him to fall back. Unbeknownst to everyone, Mack, Lil' Saint, Julian, and Lachaun were standing at the double doorway of the funeral home watching everything unfold. Tears manifested in Lachaun's eyes and she held her manicured fingers to her face. Water slicked her cheeks seeing her husband and his son reunited. The two of them hadn't seen each other for what seemed like an eternity. They hardly spoke over the phone because KiMani was always out running the streets. The young nigga was hard to get ahold of.

KiMani collided with his father and wrapped his arms around his waist. He buried his wet face into his torso and squeezed his eyes shut, fighting back tears. He considered himself a G like his father, and he didn't want to be seen as anything less in his eyes. Hellraiser's wrists were shackled, so as bad as he wanted to, he couldn't hug his son back. All he could do was take off his hood and kiss his forehead.

"I love you, Pops. I missed you so much," KiMani said, still holding tight to his father.

"I love you even more, son, and miss you just as much," Hellraiser told him.

At this time, the rain was continuously beating against everyone: Arnez, the sheriffs, Hellraiser, and KiMani. Lachaun was crying profusely and wiping her eyes with balled-up tissues.

KiMani took his face away from his father's torso. His eyes were pink and watery, but he wasn't going to cry. At least, he was still trying not to. "I want chu to come home,

Pops. That's all I want, is for you to come home."

"I've gotta few more years, but I'll—" Hellraiser was cut short by Officer Hernandez yanking KiMani out of the way and pulling him along. Officer Allen started to protest but decided to keep his mouth shut and go along.

"We've gotta go if we're gonna keep schedule," Officer Hernandez said with a scowl. He was an asshole that liked to flex his authoritative muscle every chance he got, especially when it came to brothers.

"I'll be home, Ki. I promise I'll be home, and when I do, it's me and you—we're gonna be a family—you hear me, son? A family!" Hellraiser called out to KiMani as he was pulled away. "You're gonna stay with Lachaun now! You mind her! She's gonna take care of you 'til I get home!"

"No, Pops, I don't want chu to go! I don't want chu to leave!" KiMani called out to him, dashing in his direction. Crying, he lifted up his sweatshirt and revealed a gun in his waistline. "I want chu to stay home!" KiMani was aching for the love of his father. Seeing him being ripped out of his life again peeled off the scab that had formed over his heart the from first time he was taken from him. He had it in his mind to shoot it out with the sheriffs so he could free his old man. He had a couple of sneaker boxes full of money, so he figured they could use that to escape the country. That was about as far he'd gotten with his plan. He would come up with the rest as they went along. Right now, his main concern was making a jailbreak with his pops and getting the fuck out of dodge.

Unbeknownst to KiMani, Mack, Lil' Saint, Julian, and Lachaun saw what was about to happen. They took off running down the steps to try to stop him. They were calling out for him to stop as they chased after him, fearing he was going to commit suicide with his actions. Their voices fell on deaf ears, though. And the sheriffs were too far away to hear them themselves.

"You watch after my boy, Arnez! If you love 'em the way you say you do, then you watch after my prince!" Hellraiser told him as he was ushered past him. He was a legend to Arnez and a bunch of young goons like him. They'd chopped it up on the jack a few times, and KiMani had sent a few pictures of them together.

"You got that, OG. On the set, I'ma do just that!" Arnez swore and tapped his fist against his chest.

"Leave these streets alone, son! You leave these streets alone! These streets don't love nobody—I promise you! These streets took me away from you, my baby boy, my family!" he called out as loud as he could over his shoulder. He was trying to say everything he could before he was shoved back inside of the van and whisked away.

KiMani's face twisted into a mask of hatred, and he bit down on his bottom lip. He came up from his waistline with his gun and extended in the sheriff's direction. He narrowed his eyes as the rain pelted against his face and clothing.

"KiMani, noooooooooooo!" Lachaun called out to him. She'd tripped and fell onto her hands while running, losing one of her shoes in the process. As she looked ahead, Mack, Lil' Saint, and Julian were still chasing after KiMani.

Tears streamed down KiMani's cheeks as he placed his finger upon the trigger of his gun. As he began to apply the ten pounds of pressure needed to fire the first shot, he was tackled to the spongy lawn. He fell hard on his face, and his piece flew across the ground. Mack and Julian were lying on top of him. However, Lil' Saint was searching the ground for his gun. Once he found it, he picked it up and stashed it inside of his suit jacket.

"Pops, I love you! Don't leave me, man! Don't leave

me!" KiMani cried out, tears slicking down his cheeks.

"I love you too, son! I'll be back, man! I'll be ba—" Hellraiser was cut off by Officer Hernandez's punk ass slamming the doors of the van on him. Officer Allen fired up the hulking vehicle while Officer Hernandez climbed into the front passenger seat.

"Get off me, get off of me!" KiMani hollered out at his uncles. Mack and Julian got off him. He scrambled to his feet and took off running towards the van. He shoved Arnez, who was trying to stop him, aside and kept running. He tripped and fell on the slick grass, but quickly got back up on his feet. He saw the van driving down the road. It was becoming smaller and smaller before his eyes. This drove him to run even faster than he did before.

"Don't leave me, man! Please, don't leave me! I need you! I need you!" KiMani said, darting out into the road and chasing after the van. No matter how hard he ran, he couldn't catch up with it. "I need you, Pops! Pleeeease!" He tripped over a big stone in the middle of the road and fell, busting his mouth. His grill dripped blood as he pushed up from the ground on his hands and knees. His mouth was throbbing, but he ignored the pain. That pain was nothing compared to the pain he felt in his heart.

KiMani broke down crying in the road with the rain mixing with his tears. He bowed his head. His shoulders rocked back and forth as he wept. Slowly, Mack, Lil' Saint, Julian, Lachaun, and Arnez gathered onto the cemetery road around KiMani. Lachaun consoled him like only a mother could and helped him to his feet. He abruptly hugged her and she held him. She kissed the top of his head and rubbed his back soothingly. They both stared up the road at the van. It grew smaller and smaller until it vanished before their eyes.

***

Hellraiser stared out the gated back window of the van, watching Lachaun and KiMani hold each other in the middle of the road. His face was balled up in anger and tears were oozing out of his pink eyes, slicking down his cheeks. He watched them grow smaller and smaller the further the van drove.

Hellraiser hoped like hell KiMani did what he said and left the streets alone. He didn't want to lose him to them like his mother had him and his father. He knew the chances of his boy turning his back on the game were highly unlikely, especially since he had his blood coursing through his veins. The men in his family were notoriously stubborn and ambitious. On top of that, they loved a challenge, and believed they could do anything they put their minds to.

Hellraiser looked away from the gated window and squeezed his eyes shut. His eyebrows sloped and he wrinkled his nose. He clenched and unclenched his jaws, making a fat vein throb at his temples. When he peeled his eyes back open, he looked like he'd been possessed by a demonic spirit from hell. He was on some real murder shit now. All the niggaz that owed OG a debt were going to feel his pain—tenfold! He desperately needed somebody to take his grief out on. And who better to get his wrath than the punk mothafuckaz who weren't in his pops' good graces?

***

When Hellraiser returned to prison, he was made to strip naked to perform the same procedure he had to when he returned from a visit. Afterward, he got back dressed in his state-issued uniform and shoes and was escorted down to the infirmary. The nurse on duty tested to see if he had used any

166

alcohol, drugs, or unauthorized controlled substances while he was out of the department's custody. As soon as he was cleared, he was free to return to his cell where he found OG laid back on his bunk. The old head was wearing glasses reading Sam Greenlee's *The Spook Who Sat by the Door*.

When OG saw Hellraiser enter their cell, he sat his book aside on his bunk and pulled off his glasses. He jumped down to the floor and approached him. He could tell by the look on his face he was feeling some type of way, so he went to hug him. Hellraiser held his hand to the old man's chest, stopping him in his tracks. OG's forehead wrinkled, wondering why his son was denying him.

"I don't need that right now, Pops," Hellraiser assured him. "Right now, I'm on some real goon shit, and I don't need love. That love shit gon' have a nigga in his feelings."

"I understand, son." OG nodded. "I understand."

"Good. Right now, I need you to watch the door for me," he told him, violence twinkling in his eyes. "I saw that bitch-ass nigga Dabo on my way up here. I'm finna sharpen my shit a lil' bit, then I'ma get at his hoe ass."

"Son, you don't have to do that r—"

"Nah, fuck that, Pops. I ain't even tryna hear it," Hellraiser said sternly. "That nigga playing witcho grips, so now he's gotta feel it. Now hold down the door!"

OG nodded understandingly, knowing his son wanted to relieve some of that pent-up anger inside of him. He and his grandson, KiMani, were exactly like him. They all had damn near the same personality. The way he saw it, if putting some steel up in a nigga was going to make his boy feel better, then he was willing to let him go along with the deadly task.

OG posted up inside the doorway of their cell and folded his arms across his chest. He looked up and down the tier to make sure there wasn't anyone coming. There wasn't anyone in sight, so he played it cool, keeping a watchful eye out.

Shink, shink, shink, shink, shink!

The sound of metal being swept back and forth across the cement floor resonated inside of the cell. Hellraiser left hundreds of white scratch lines on the surface from where he sharpened his shank. Although the blade was already sharp, he wanted it sharper so he wouldn't have any problems putting it through his intended target.

Suddenly, Hellraiser stopped sharpening his shank and looked at it. He blew off whatever residue was on the prison-fashioned knife and brushed off the rest of it. He pressed his thumb against the tip of it, and a bubble of blood formed. He smiled devilishly in satisfaction at the lethal weapon he'd crafted. Hellraiser stood upright and thrust the blade in different directions, imagining himself stabbing up Dabo.

Hellraiser stopped shadow fighting with the prison-fashioned knife and looked at it admiringly. Wiping the sprinkles of sweat from his forehead, he hid the shank on him and pulled a one-hundred-dollar bill from the hole inside his mattress. He folded the crisp Benjamin Franklin into a square and placed it inside of his palm, flexing it.

"I'll be back," Hellraiser told his pops as he passed him, pulling on his nose.

Arms still folded across his chest, OG watched his son step out onto the tier and head toward his destination confidently. He already knew what trouble lay ahead for homeboy that owed him money. But life was all about the choices you make, and he wasn't about to allow himself to feel sorry for a grown-ass man that made the wrong ones.

When Hellraiser reached the landing from the tier's stairs, he made a right and walked past the same CO that had escorted him to the infirmary. The entire walk to the infirmary, they discussed him turning off the surveillance cameras for a price. The deal was a hundred bucks.

Hellraiser discreetly passed the corrections officer his payment as they crossed paths. He strolled by a couple of convicts talking shit and horsing around. He was so incognito they hadn't even noticed him, and that was exactly how he wanted it. Hellraiser's eyes zeroed in on Dabo's cell. The closer he neared it, the more he scanned his surroundings. There weren't any eyes on him, so he knew he was clear to handle his business. He turned into Dabo's cell and found him with his back to him. He was standing over the commode relieving his swollen bladder.

"Whooo, goddamn, bruh, dat White Lightnin' gotta nigga pissin' like a Brahma bull," Dabo said to no one particular, holding his limp meat and pissing inside the toilet bowl.

Hellraiser pulled his shank from where he had it hidden. He hunched down with his prison knife poised to attack, moving in on his target like a keen panther. Dabo, looking down at his dick, shook the dripping piss from it. He was in the middle of putting it away when he saw a shadow closing in from behind him. His eyes got as big as baseballs and his mouth flew open. His dick was still hanging freely when he whipped around to defend himself. By the time he was facing Hellraiser, he was rushing him with blinding speed. Hellraiser pressed his forearm against Dabo's throat and forced him up against the wall, knocking over nearby items.

Dabo made an ugly, pained face, bumping his head against the wall. When he saw Hellraiser's face, he knew what time it was and what this situation was about.

"Say, bruh, I got dat fa OG, I got—"

"I don't give a fuck!" Hellraiser barked harshly and sprayed his face with spit. His eyes were an evil red and his face was a mask of hatred. He was in full beast mode now! He looked like a straight-up savage! "Here comes the pain!"

Hellraiser slammed his shank down into Dabo's right eye and pulled it out. Homeboy hollered out in agony, but that didn't stop his blood-thirsty attacker. Hellraiser pulled the prison-made knife out of his eye and slammed it into his cheek, over and over again. He then slammed his blade into Dabo's neck and chest. The brutality of the attack dotted his face and uniform with blood. Still pressing his forearm against Dabo's neck, Hellraiser poked him in his torso fifty times. The fist balled around the shank was like a blur, it was moving so fast.

"Where the fuck the bag at, nigga, huh? Fuck the money at?" Hellraiser said, evil dripping down his face. His nostrils were flared and his teeth were clenched. He was now standing over Dabo, who was sitting on the floor and holding his bleeding eye.

"Over there, bruh! Over there!" Dabo told him, jabbing his finger at the toiletries his money was hidden in. Hellraiser knocked over several hygiene products in his search for the items that Dabo stashed his loot in. The items fell to the floor, making a chaotic sound and rolling in every direction.

"Which deodorant, nigga?" Hellraiser asked, turning around to him holding two sticks of deodorant. One was Speed Stick and the other was Suave.

"The—the Speed Stick!" Dabo told him, pointing at the deodorant in his right hand. "I was finna come up dere and holla at OG, bruh. I swear 'fore God, I was gon' pay 'em," he claimed, watching Hellraiser pop open the Speed Stick. He removed the green see-through deodorant stick and smiled at what he found inside. He tapped the contents out into his palm. It was two small, wrinkled up bankrolls secured by rubber bands. Hellraiser stuffed the bankrolls into his pocket. Curious as to what was inside of the Suave deodorant, he popped its lid and pulled out its stick also.

There were two small bankrolls there as well.

"Wait a minute—wait a minute, bruh! You taking mo' then I o—Ooof!" Dabo's face balled up in pain and he fell to the side, holding himself. Hellraiser had pocketed the bankrolls from the Suave deodorant and kicked him in his stomach.

"Shut the fuck up, ol' country-ass nigga! I'm taking that for taking me through all this, when you know how I get down for mine!" Hellraiser told him with fury written over his face. He grabbed Dabo by the front of his uniform and forced him up against the wall. Hellraiser pressed the tip of his prison-made knife into the side of Dabo's neck, and blood oozed out of it. A bubble of blood formed and slid down like a teardrop. Dabo's eyes were stretched wide open in fear. He swallowed the ball of nervousness in his throat and held up his hands.

"Okay, okay, bruh, you got it. You got it," Dabo said submissively, his hands trembling. He thought he was going to get over on OG because he was an old man, but he'd been sadly mistaken.

"I know I got it, nigga! 'Cause youza poodle and I'ma pit bull that'll bite cho mothafucking head off!" Hellraiser assured him. His malevolent eyes were peering into the windows of Dabo's soul, and he didn't see a drop of gangsta in him. Dude was as soft as baby shit! "Now, listen, if I find out chu went jacking to dem boyz about this, I'ma carve yo' tongue out." He released Dabo's neck, opened his mouth, and pulled his tongue out as far as he could. Hellraiser then placed his shank to the side of it. He smiled wickedly. "You hear me, pussy nigga? Huh?"

"Unh huh, unh huh!" Dabo's eyes stretched open wider as he replied. He nodded in agreement.

"Good!" Hellraiser said and punched him in the eye he'd

stabbed him in. He flew across the cell and the side of his head deflected off the commode. He balled up on the floor, holding his aching eye with one hand and his wounded torso with the other.

Hellraiser came out of Dabo's cell, making hurried footsteps and glancing over his shoulder. The same convicts he saw on his way into his victim's cell were still horsing around. He was glad they weren't paying any attention to him whatsoever. He may as well have been a ghost as far as they were concerned. Hellraiser casually walked up the steps to the top tier where he was housed. As he walked toward his cell, he looked over the guard rail and saw one of the niggaz that was horsing around headed to Dabo's cell.

"Oh, shit!" he overheard the homeboy say when he entered the cell. A minute later, he came running out and past the other convicts. "CO! CO! CO!" he called out over and over again for the corrections officer, waving his hand. The other convicts he was horsing around with had followed him. Their faces were most likely frowned with concern, wondering what had happened.

Hellraiser disappeared into the cell and stripped off his shirt. He cut it to shreds, flushing it and his shank down the toilet easily. He tossed OG, who was lying on his bunk reading *The Spook Who Sat by the Door* again, the debt Dabo owed him and rushed over to the sink. He looked at the metal reflector at the dots of blood covering his face. He turned on the faucet and cupped his hands underneath the cool flowing water. He splashed it against his face back to back, rinsing it off completely. He then washed the blood from his hands and threw on another uniform shirt.

Right then, the alarm sounded for lockdown. That's when Hellraiser knew one of the COs had seen what he'd done to Dabo. Quickly, he grabbed one of the books his father had on deck and laid back on his bunk. His face was still wet from splashing water on it and his heart was thudding from the mission. But he was playing it cool, reading the book, like he hadn't almost caught a body.

After doing what he did to blow off some steam, Hellraiser was positive KiMani was out in the streets doing the same thing. He just prayed that if he was committing violence, it was against someone that undoubtedly deserved it.

***

That night

KiMani managed to get himself together after the emotional departure from his father. The pallbearers were coming out of the funeral home with Big Ma's coffin to deposit it into the ground. He was going to allow her handlers to follow through with the ritual, but Lachaun convinced him to take one last look at her. Under the minister's orders, the pallbearers took the coffin back inside of the funeral home and let KiMani have some time alone with his grandmother.

The moment he found himself face to face with Big Ma's corpse, KiMani regretted allowing Lachaun to talk him into saying his final goodbyes to her. He broke down crying and threw himself on top of Big Ma. His shoulders shook as he sobbed his eyes out. His teardrops dropped from his cheeks and slicked her face wet. Having heard his sobs, Lachaun opened the double doors of the funeral home to see what was going on. As soon as she did, KiMani darted down the aisle, past her and into the cold night's air. He hopped into the passenger seat of Arnez's whip where he was waiting for him, and he pulled off.

Arnez and KiMani copped an ounce of Grand Daddy Kush and a couple more bottles of Cristal. They posted up with some bitchez and some niggaz they knew in The Jungles, getting loaded. Arnez winded up dipping off with one of the broads for some cutty. Two of the girls tried to get something popping with KiMani, but he wasn't in the mood. He was still hurt and angry about the passing of Big Ma. And the fact that he wouldn't see his old man for at least another five years.

KiMani was sitting in the front passenger seat of Arnez's whip with his leg hanging out of the door. He and another nigga he knew on the strength of Arnez were passing a blunt between them and chopping it up. Well, actually, it was homeboy that was doing all of the talking. KiMani was more so half listening.

The Relatives' "Slide Like This" was pumping out of the whip's speakers, making the entire ride thump like a marathon runner's heart. Two of the homegirls were sitting on the hood of Arnez's ride sharing one of the bottles of Cristal. A third one, whose hair was done in red individual braids, was already drunk and high. She held a red bandana in her hand while she did the blood walk. The two chicks sitting on the hood of the car cheered her on. In fact, one of them hopped off the hood and ran over to join her on the sidewalk.

"Aye, aye, aye, get it, bitch! Go, bitch, get it, bitch, aye, aye!" the girl shouted from the hood, holding up the 300-dollar bottle of champagne.

Two of the homies from The Jungles were leaning up against the trunk of Arnez's ride. They were getting drunk and high as well. Once they heard old girl cheering from the hood and holding up the bottle of champagne, they sat their cups of alcohol down and mashed out what was left of the blunt they were smoking. Afterward, they came up behind the girls and they started winding and grinding on them. Wanting to get in on the action, homegirl with the bottle of Cristal hopped down from the hood and ran over to the sidewalk. She danced up behind one of the niggaz that was holding her homegirl by her waist. He moved his body in sync with the chick in the front of him while holding the ass of the one in back of him. The broad in the back of him guzzled some more of the Cristal. Old boy tilted his head back and she smiled sexily, pouring the champagne inside of his mouth. He swallowed it, licked his lips, and kissed her hungrily.

"Look at these bitchez, Blood," the nigga in the car with KiMani said and nudged him. He looked through the windshield at his homies and homegirls, pointing them out to KiMani. "I don't know what it is about weed and alcohol but, on the gang, it gets these bitchez going!"

"Hell, yeah," KiMani replied with a weak smile. He wasn't interested at all in the show playing out before him.

Old boy in the car with him took another hit of the blunt and passed it back to KiMani. He then cranked the volume up on the song and hopped out of the car. He darted over to where everyone was dancing and started dancing up on the broad that was blood walking. Instantly, she began bumping and grinding on him. He held her waist with one hand and threw his hood up with the other.

KiMani saw movement from the corner of his right eye and looked in that direction. He saw Arnez coming down the stairway of an apartment complex he'd entered with the girl he'd left with earlier. Arnez was making hurried footsteps down the stairs, holding a gun and the waist of his sagging sweatpants in one hand. He was using his free hand to slip his arm inside the sleeve of his hoodie.

"Yo', Lil' Hell, man, we've gotta roll!" Arnez called out to him. "It's popping in the h—" He was cut short as he fell to the ground, pulling up his sweatpants. Scrambling back up on his sneakers, he yanked his sweats back up his waist and tucked his piece. He ran out of the gate, looking both ways before jogging across the street. "Aye, Blood, we'll have to kick it with y'all later. We've got business to attend to." He dapped up a couple of the homeboys and jumped in behind the wheel. KiMani threw what was left of the blunt to the asphalt, pulled his leg in, and slammed the door shut. Right then, Arnez was firing up his ride and peeling off, carrying The Relatives' "Slide Like This" along with him.

"Yo, Blood, what's up?" a frowning KiMani asked curiously, sitting up in the passenger seat.

"Niggaz shot up the homie Zekey's momma's crib!" Arnez told him as he zoomed through traffic. All of the windows were down and the air was blowing inside of the car. The forceful winds disturbed his and KiMani's hair and ruffled their clothing.

"For what?" KiMani asked, frowning further.

"From what the homie said, he was standing outside talking to his bitch and fools drove by blasting. They missed him, but laid his broad down!" Arnez said, eyes focused on the windshield. "Nigga sounded like he'd been crying, so I know he fucked up! My nigga, Zekey, doesn't cry. Homie doesn't have a heart."

KiMani nodded his understanding of Zekey. It was true. That coldhearted mothafucka didn't have a heart. He only cared about getting high, his momma, and causing destruction. That's right. He lived to put in work! So much so, that when there wasn't any drama, he'd start something just to have something to do.

"You can say that again," KiMani replied. "So what's the move?"

"We gon' dip to my spot, get dressed for the occasion, and grab some blowers," he informed him. "Then we gon' slide up to General Hospital and snatch this fool Zekey up."

KiMani and anyone else involved in the streets knew about Zekey and how he played the game. He was a low-down, grimy nigga known for gunplay and fucking fools over. Especially if it meant he stood to benefit from it! KiMani didn't fuck with homeboy at all. He didn't care for him because he was conniving and unpredictable. You never knew what his narcissistic ass was up to or what he was scheming on. Arnez, on the other hand, had mad love for homeboy, though. And based on the fact that Zekey had become his mentor and sponsored him into the set, KiMani couldn't blame him. They had an uncle and nephew kind of bond, so he knew Arnez would never stop fucking with dude.

I already know what time it is if we're going to pick up the guns and scoop up this 51/50 nigga. We're gon' roll on whoever them fools was that shot up dude's momma's house! I don't rock with the OG, but on the strength of my nigga, Arnez, I'ma roll! Besides, I'm not gon' feel any better 'til I body something! Damn, that shit sounds crazy as fuck, Blood! I'm not gon' feel any better 'til I blow down an opps, KiMani thought, shaking his head and feeling ashamed. This killa shit really was coursing through a young nigga's veins. *I wonder if Pops and his old man feel how I feel, if putting something to sleep makes 'em feel better. If so, then all of the men in our family sick and need help.*

KiMani's mind was weighed heavily with the thoughts of his loved ones. The hurt and anger he felt inside hadn't subsided. He was a ticking time bomb ready to explode. He needed a release and he needed one fast. This mission he was about to go on would prove to be just the remedy for his heartache and turmoil.

Chapter Twelve

KiMani and Arnez dipped by his crib. They got dressed in all black, grabbed black Nike baseball gloves, and loaded up their guns. They took an extra pair of gloves, three black baseball caps, three full-face neoprene masks, and an additional pair of black clothes. They left Arnez's crib and swung by General Hospital to pick up that nigga, Zekey. Arnez hit him up while they waited for him in the parking lot. A couple of minutes later, a six-foot-one, muscle-bound man emerged out of the double doors of the hospital. He looked around for Arnez's whip, but he didn't see him. Arnez waved him over and honked the horn at the exact same time.

Zekey perked up when he saw Arnez waving him over in his direction. He walked through the dark parking lot with a terrifying edge that gave those watching him Jason Voorhees vibes. When he was finally up on Arnez's whip, Arnez and KiMani got a good look at him. He was a hunk of a man with a shiny bald head and a five o'clock shadow. He was wearing a white T-shirt underneath a soft gray hoodie and matching sweatpants. All of which were stained with the blood of his woman, Yoyo. She'd gotten caught in the crossfire when fools drove by chopping up his mother's crib. His eyes were red webbed and glassy while his nose was the color of a rose petal. Arnez and KiMani couldn't figure out if he'd been crying over the loss of his loved one, or if he was high off the bags of dope he was known to have on him.

Zekey snatched open the door and deposited himself in the backseat. He greeted Arnez and KiMani, and they threw their heads back like, *What's up?* Arnez pulled to the end of the exit, looked both ways, hit his turn signal, and made a left turn. He looked back and forth between the windshield and the rearview mirror at Zekey. He saw him dip his head and snort something up his nose. Arnez knew how he got down, so it was obvious he was snorting dope. Arnez and KiMani exchanged glances but acted like they didn't know what he was doing back there.

This nigga, Zekey, is a bold mothafucka! How the fuck he just gon' hop inna backseat of my whip and start shoveling that shit up his nose? Unc ain't got no shame! He really doesn't give a fuck, Arnez thought. He glanced in the rearview mirror again to see Zekey throwing his head back and pulling on his nose. He then rubbed it, snorted, and made an annoying ass sound with his throat.

"Unc!" Arnez called him.

"Huh?" Zekey said with glassy, hooded eyes that resembled Forest Whitaker's. He went to grip his gun, but then he remembered he'd buried it in his mother's yard so the cops wouldn't find it.

"Relax, my nigga, you're good," Arnez assured him, trying to calm his nerves. "You're riding in here with us. We're family. You're safe."

Speak for yo'self, Arnez, this mothafucking dopehead ain't my family, KiMani thought as he focused his attention out of the passenger window. He busied himself watching the streets whip past him.

Upon hearing Arnez say this, Zekey relaxed a little and dug in his nose. Arnez watched him the entire time, shaking his head. The nigga whose G he saluted was a certified dopefiend. It made him feel ashamed to call him family, but then he thought about how he'd saved him from becoming food in the streets. No one looked out for him like Zekey had. Homie didn't have to do that because he wasn't of his bloodline, and he didn't owe him shit. It was because of this he was willing to give his life to him on a silver platter.

"Unc, tell me again what happened at Mom's crib," Arnez said.

"Like I said, I was in the front yard arguing with Yoyo's ass, and the next thang I know, mothafucking Mexicans slid through busting them choppaz!" Zekey told him. "Them wetbacks chopped up my mom's crib, tore up the steps, the garage door, and her Bui..." He nodded a few times and then bowed his head, snoring. Saliva pooled in his mouth and poured out of the corner of it, soiling his sweatpants.

"Unc, Unc, Unc!" Arnez called after him again and again. Each time he called, he got louder and louder. "This mothafucka done dozed off again," he said under his breath. He looked at KiMani and he was shaking his head. "What?"

"Nothing, bruh, absolutely fucking nothing," KiMani said as he ran his hand down his face and expelled air.

Arnez stopped at a red stoplight, put his whip in park, and leaned over into the backseat. He shook Zekey's leg roughly to wake him up, but he wouldn't budge. He was still drooling and snoring like nothing had happened.

"Alright, I bet this wake yo' ass up!" Arnez claimed. He drew his open hand above his shoulder and swung it around with all his might—*smack*! He went across Zekey's cheek, stinging it. He came back around with his open hand—*smack*!

"What the fuck?" Zekey blurted and started swinging, thinking someone was attacking him. He dropped his arms and looked around wide-eyed with his mouth hanging open.

"Man, wake yo' old ass up and finish telling us what the fuck happened back at Dorothea's house," Arnez told him with aggravation in his voice.

"Yo, Arnez, the light's green," KiMani alerted him, tapping him on his arm.

Arnez deposited himself back into the driver's seat, strapped his safety belt back across him, and threw his Chevy Impala in drive. He took off across the light, looking into the rearview mirror at Zekey, who was smacking himself in the face with both hands. He was trying his best to stay awake.

Arnez was the only nigga on the face of the planet that could get away with handling Zekey the way he had. Had it been anyone else that came at him like that, he would have blown their brains on the dashboard.

"You up now, nigga?" Arnez asked as he drove through the streets, taking in the scenery.

"Yeah, I'm up, nephew," Zekey assured him. "But, yeah, the eses rolled through blasting, and Yoyo's dumbass fucked around and got hit. I clapped back, blew out a couple of windows and put two through the passenger side door. I don't think I took none of them fools off the shelf, though."

"Why they coming at cho neck, though?" KiMani finally spoke up. He was sure it was more to the story than Zekey was telling. It was always some fishy shit in any situation he was associated with.

"Man, it's that nigga Changa's nephew, Travieso," Zekey told him. "I was in a dice game with that fool and a couple of his homies. I started hitting their asses up. Them fools felt some type of way 'cause I told 'em I was done gambling. Travieso started wolfing shit, so I fired on his ass, busted 'em right in his grill. Soon as I dropped him, the rest of his punk-ass homeboys packed me out. I came up off the hip with my shit spitting, tryna lay all them wet backs down. I only managed to hit one of them in the ribs, the rest of 'em got away."

"How they know where yo' mom's stay, though?" Arnez asked.

"Mannnnn, I don't know. My only guess is them fools seen me out there with Yoyo and took advantage of the opportunity."

Arnez nodded his head. Zekey's story made sense, so he was going to roll with him.

"You know where to find this fool, Unc?" Arnez inquired, glancing at his street uncle through the rearview mirror.

"Yeah, I know exactly where that nigga be at, Blood," Zekey said. "My lil' Mexican bitch stay across the street from 'em. I seen 'em in and outta his grandma's house a few times. He be serving big dope at the back of that mothafucka. Crazy shit about it, nephew, there's always some lil' kids and shit over there. I think he using them as a cover up thinking The Ones won't suspect 'em of slinging outta there."

"Yo, Unc, bang yo' bitch line and see if that fool Travieso's over there," Arnez told him.

"Alright," Zekey replied and pulled out his cellular. He hit up his little Mexican broad for the info. Three minutes later, he was promising to come see her and disconnecting the call. "Yeah, him and the rest of them fools are there."

"Alright, we on them niggaz then," Arnez said. He stole a glance at KiMani and could tell his mind was somewhere else. "Yo, Blood, you can sit this one out if you want. I won't hold it against you. Me and Unc got this."

"Nah, I'm with it," KiMani assured him. "If one ride, then we all ride."

"My nigga." Arnez smiled and dapped him up. Right after, their moment was interrupted by Zekey snorting that shit up his nose. Arnez and KiMani exchanged glances and shook their heads. "Unc, what's the deal with Yoyo? Is she gonna pull through?"

Zekey pulled his head back up and wiped the heroin residue from his nostrils. He cleared his throat and replied, "She's dead."

"Damn," Arnez said, shaking his head once again. He really felt for Yoyo. He crossed himself in the sign of the holy crucifix and continued to whip down the road.

Vrooom!

Arnez's Chevrolet Impala zipped down the street through the traffic light right before it turned red.

***

Las Vegas/Penthouse Suite

Hitt-Man held her ass cheeks apart as he pounded away at her warm, gooey center. Her twat occasionally farted with each of his thrusts, and a ripple traveled up her chunky bottom. The smell of sex and the sound of clapping filled the air every time his hot, sweaty body collided with hers.

"Ahhh, fuck, faster, faster!" the Somalian dimepiece called out in between eating his wife's pussy. Her head and her perfectly shaped, dark-brown areola breasts bounced up and down with each plunge of Hitt-Man's thick endowment. The dopeman's dick glistened from the flow of her womb's natural secretions.

"Ssssssss," Niqua hissed like a venomous serpent while dimepiece was sucking on the small flap of meat nestled between her sex lips. The spectacular sensation was driving her wild. She could literally feel the muscles of her kitty contracting and spilling its juices. "Mmmmmm! Yes, yessss, fuck!" she egged on the bitch that was sucking on her clit and fingering her. She clenched and unclenched her jaws, which caused veins to bulge on her forehead. "Ah, ah, ah,

184

ah!" She humped into her mouth and then bit down on her bottom lip.

Niqua was a chocolate goddess that held an uncanny resemblance to Keisha in the movie *Belly*, except her tits and ass were enhanced thanks to the best plastic surgeon in Beverly Hills. Shorty was inked from her neck, to her arms, to her thighs. Her navel and clit were pierced with genuine diamonds. All of these attributes accompanied by her short Cleopatra hairstyle and Egyptian style of makeup made her look like the African American female rappers of today.

Niqua licked her full lips and manipulated one of her nipples since her other hand was holding a bottle of Cristal. She looked down at shorty that was giving her dome and then back up at Hitt-Man. Watching her husband dick down the bitch eating her pussy turned her the fuck on. She couldn't get enough of the shit! He puckered his lips up at her and she puckered hers back up at him. She guzzled some of the champagne, spilling it down her chin. She wiped it away and looked down at the dimepiece who was feasting on her treasure. She poured some of the tasty liquid on her flat stomach. It formed a small river as it flowed down her torso and washed over her vagina. The Somalian dimepiece sucked up some of the bubbly, but Hitt-Man was stroking her so good she looked back at him.

"Just like that! Oh, yes, just like that!" the Somalian dimepiece hollered as Hitt-Man sped up his back shots. His locs bounced as he moved his hips back and forth. The wet clapping sound grew louder and louder, and the smell of sex became heavier inside the suite.

The two million dollars in icy gold jewelry bounced up and down on Hitt-Man's shiny, tattooed chest. Sweat leaped from his muscular form and splashed upon her back and ass. The dopeman had a mad dog expression on his face as he plowed into the dimepiece. He smacked her on her booty again, then he sucked on his thumb, making sure it was nice and dripping with his spit. Without warning, he shoved it up the dimepiece's asshole and drew a sensual whine from her.

"You like that shit, huh?" Hitt-Man asked as he watched himself go in and out of the Somalian dimepiece's twat. She was cumming so much that white shit was coating more and more of his dick.

"Oh, yes, yes! I like it, I fucking love it!" the Somalian dimepiece called out with a jovial look on her face. Hitt-Man continued to give it to her, that gangsta dick raw and uncut like he knew her old rat ass liked it. He looked up at Niqua with his locs hanging over his face. All she could see past his locs were his tormenting eyes. They made him look like a straightup beast. She held his intense gaze while he continued to beat that dime bitch's back up.

Hitt-Man knew how much his wife got off to him smashing bitchez in front of her. That shit made her horny enough to bust on the spot! Niqua's hardened nipples and erect clit made this apparent.

"Ah, ah, ah, ah, fuck, y—yes!" The Somalian dimepiece's eyes rolled and her mouth hung open. Hitt-Man saw she wasn't eating his wife's pussy, and that made him mad. He loved busting down a new bitch, but he enjoyed it more knowing his wife was being satisfied too.

"Bitch, shut the fuck up and eat my queen's pussy!" Hitt-Man demanded and mashed her face into his wife's bald twat. He grinned wickedly seeing Niqua squirm and lick her lips, enjoying getting her clit manipulated. She wrapped her legs around the dimepiece's neck. The bitch was sucking on her jewel, fingering her savagely while rubbing on her own shit.

Ain't no fun if wifey can't have none, Hitt-Man thought, looking at the pleasured expression written across his queen's face.

"That's right, ho, eat my shit—eat this pussy!" Niqua whined sensually, rotating her hips and tweaking her nipple. She passed the bottle of Cristal to her husband and focused on her nipples. Her pretty, French tip-manicured toes curled, and her eyes rolled back. Niqua, using her diamond-pierced tongue, licked her top row of teeth erotically. "Uh, uh, uh, uh, uh, uh!" She grabbed a handful of the Somalian dime-piece's hair and threw her head back. She could feel her orgasm building up and up. It felt like she had to piss really, really bad, but that definitely wasn't the case. Niqua stared up at their reflections courtesy of the mirrored ceiling. She observed her husband pour champagne on the bitch they were flipping back and then drink from it thirstily.

Hitt-Man switched hands with the Cristal bottle and occasionally smacked the Somalian dimepiece on her ass as he stroked her from the back. More sweat oozed out of his pores, sliding down his chest, rock-hard abs, and hairy muscular buttocks.

"Yeah, bitch, eat the royal pussy while the king fucks you from the back!" Hitt-Man commanded and gave her butt another hard smack. Her ass cheek jiggled and a red hand impression appeared. Holding the bottle in his hand, he fucked her from the back faster and made her booty jump. The faster he attacked her from that angle, the wetter she got and the harder she rubbed her clit.

"Uh, uh, uh, uh!" the Somalian dimepiece hollered out with a scrunched face.

"Oooooh, oh! Oh! Oh, shiiit!" Niqua's faced balled up in bliss and she mashed that bitch's face back into her pussy.

"Eat me, bitch! Eat me!" Niqua urged her. She could feel her orgasm coming ahead, and her legs were shaking. Her ghetto, sexy ass looked like a volcano on the verge of erupting. "I'm 'bouta cum, I'm 'bouta cum!"

"Mmmmmm—Mmmmmm!" the Somalian dimepiece said with a mouthful of Niqua's phat pussy. Shorty was trying to say 'I'm 'bouta cum' like Niqua. The queen was holding her in place now. She couldn't move an inch and she wasn't going to until little mama popped off.

"Shit, this pussy tight! On Blood gang, I'm 'bouta bust!" Hitt-Man claimed, balling his face. He could feel his nuts swelling and semen building in his shit. The penthouse suite filled with moans and groans of all the participants in the threesome. The closer they all got to getting off, the louder the moans and groans became, until they exploded.

"Aaaahh, fuuuuuuck!" Niqua hollered out and sprayed the dimepiece's face. She then fell flat out on the bed. Her eyes were narrowed and her mouth was open. Her entire body shook like she was a death-row inmate in an electric chair.

"Shhiiiiiiit!" the Somalian dimepiece hollered with bulging eyes and a wide-open mouth. Her juices flooded her thighs as she reached her orgasm. She started shaking just like Niqua and fell flat on her stomach. That didn't stop Hitt-Man from climbing on top of her and placing his fists on either side of her. He pumped her six fast, hard times and bust deep inside of her. Warm, clear globs of his gooey semen splashed against her pink walls. Exhausted, he fell on the side of her on the bed. He lay there hot and sweaty with a thudding heart and semi-hard dick.

"Goddamn. That shit hit the spot!" Hitt-Man emphasized 'spot' and smacked the dimepiece on her ass. She jumped from the sting of the smack, whimpered, and started dozing off to sleep. "What's up, queen? How was it?" He looked toward the head of the bed at Niqua.

"Shit was decent," Niqua replied, exhausted, with a thudding heart. She sat up, looked at homegirl while she was snoring, and kicked that bitch out of the bed. She hollered in freefall before she collided with the carpeted floor. "It's time for you to go, love."

Niqua hopped out of bed and slipped on her kimono, tying it around her waist. She left the bedroom and came back with a glass of water and a Plan-B pill. When she returned, Hitt-Man was sitting on the edge of the bed while old girl was climbing back up on her bare feet.

"Here you go." Niqua passed her the glass and the pill. She folded her arms across her chest and tapped her foot impatiently. She eyeballed homegirl as she tossed back the pill and washed it down. The girl sat the empty glass down on the nightstand and turned to Niqua, asking for her money for the sex. "Hol' up."

Niqua walked around the bed and tilted the chick's head back. Using her finger, she felt around inside of her mouth and then looked down inside of it. She didn't see the pill.

"Alright. You can get dressed," Niqua told her as she walked away. She put in the combination to the black safe that came with their room and it opened automatically. Inside, there were stacks and stacks of blue faces with rubber bands around them. She snatched out one and closed the safe. She then took the rubber band from around the dead presidents and counted off two gees. Niqua folded it and held it out to homegirl as she approached her while the girl was slipping on her pump. She took it and placed it inside of her bra.

"I'll show you out," Niqua told her as she guided her toward the door.

"Wait, here's my card." The dimepiece gave her a black business card in case she wanted her services again. Niqua glanced at it and continued to guide her toward the door. Once she saw the girl out, she shut and locked the door behind her.

Niqua tore up the black card as she journeyed towards the bedroom. She threw the tore up pieces of card into the trash can. She and Hitt-Man never flipped the same bitchez twice. That was never any fun. As she crossed the threshold of the bedroom, she could hear the shower running. She shook her head when she noticed her husband's pile of necklaces, watches, bracelets, and rings on the nightstand. For some strange reason, he enjoyed fucking while rocking all of this jewels. He called it Rich Sex, which made no fucking sense to her.

I done told this ol' big head husband of mine to keep his money and jewels inside the safe. The maids at these hotels have the keys to get into the guests' rooms, and these bitchez be stealing shit! Let's not forget those fools that were scoping us out down at the craps table earlier tonight. Dwayne thinks they were eyeballing me, but something tells me they were peeping all the chips he'd racked up and all the ice he was rocking. You can't tell his big ass shit, though. Ughh! Men! Niqua thought as she deposited her man's jewelry inside the safe along with the stacks of dead presidents. She shut the door to the safe and made her way toward the bathroom. As soon as she crossed the threshold, she peeled off her robe and hung it on the hook on the back of the door. The bathroom was humid and foggy from the hot water spraying from the shower nozzle.

Niqua shut the bathroom door and made her way toward the glass enclosure that housed the shower. The glass was running with beads of water and it was foggy. She could still make out Hitt-Man's nakedness as he lathered himself up with soap. Niqua opened the door of the shower and stepped in. She took the loofa from her man and went about the task of washing him up. He shut his eyes and bowed his head. He then placed his hands on the wall and allowed her to cater to him like the street king he was.

Hitt-Man was a multi-millionaire since Caleb was no longer in the picture. He continued to push his poison in the street until it was all gone. Then he collected the profit he'd made from it, added the dollars to it he had put up and the loot Caleb had in his secret stash. He went to the same Chinese restaurant to holla at Wang Lei and got the run around. A day later, Wang contacted him. They met up at another location and made a deal for four hundred birds of that raw. After that night, Hitt-Man took off and never looked back. He had more money than he knew what to do with and an army of assassins at his disposal.

"Baby, turn around for me so I can get cho front," Niqua told him. As soon as he did, she started lathering up his rock-hard body.

"Don't forget to clean the royal dick while you're at it," Hitt-Man told her, watching her scrub every inch of his body.

"Yes, king," Niqua replied, washing up his dick and balls. She frowned, noticing the faraway look in his eyes. "What's wrong?"

"You know, it's crazy, they say God works in mysterious ways," Hitt-Man began. "I prayed to 'em to show me a way to get rich. With the death of my best friend, I winded up taking over his business. Now, here I am—a millionaire hood nigga. I got cars, clothes, jewels up the ass, flying in private jets, and fucking the women of other niggaz dreams," he claimed as the hot liquid rinsed the soap from off his form.

"Lemme guess, you'd give it all up to have your best friend back?" Niqua asked before she started sucking on his nut sack and jerking his dick.

Hitt-Man closed his eyes and held his head back. He licked his lips and began moaning upon feeling Niqua's juicy mouth on his piece. He thought about what she'd asked him before she started giving fellatio. Would he give up all he'd obtained so Caleb could be alive again?

No! Hell no! I love this shit, Hitt-Man thought, grunting as he was getting his dick sucked. He looked down at Niqua, and she was staring at him while she fingered herself. He put his hand on her head and started fucking her mouth aggressively.

"Ack, ack, ack, ack!" Niqua gagged and choked.

***

As Arnez drove, Zekey pulled off his bloody clothes and changed into the murder gear given to him. He pulled the full-face neoprene mask over his face and turned the black baseball cap on his head backward. Next, he pulled the black gloves over his hands and flexed his fingers in them. Arnez and KiMani pulled their neoprene masks over their faces and their black gloves over their hands.

"This it right here!" Zekey blurted as they drove past a two-story white house with a black iron gate. There were four little Mexican girls in the yard. They didn't look any older than six or seven years old. Three of them were jumping rope while the fourth one stood by watching and licking her ice cream cone.

"Yo, it's kids outside, let's handle this some other time,"

KiMani said after he and Arnez saw the little girls playing in the front yard of the house they were going to hit.

"Mannnn, fuck them kids! Nephew, bust a bitch," Zekey told Arnez. "Travieso is there too. I saw his Chevy Styleline in the driveway."

Arnez busted a U-turn in the middle of the residential street and headed back in the direction of Travieso's grandmother's crib.

KiMani scowled behind his neoprene mask and clenched his jaws. He felt like pistol whipping Zekey's ass, but he knew if he did that he'd have to kill him next. Zekey was a straight-up head busta, and he wouldn't be able to live that beating down, especially if it was coming from a little nigga. It didn't even matter that he was building quite the reputation as a killa. The move would undoubtedly play on Zekey's ego because he was just a fourteen-year-old kid.

"Alright, check this out, Zekey," KiMani began, looking over his shoulder into the backseat at him. He couldn't believe Arnez was back there snorting up another bag of dope. He wanted to snap, but he held it down and kept with what was on his mind. "If we gon' bust this move, then let's bust this move. We're not killing any kids or old people. They're off limits! We gon' split ya boy Travieso's wig and whomever else is out there with 'em. Understand?"

"Lil' nigga, who the fuck you think you're talking to? I'm the OG here!" Zekey told him with animosity dripping from every word. "I don't give a fuck if Jesus and his twelve apostles are out there! Them mothafuckaz is getting it too. Straight like that!"

KiMani smacked the fifty-round drum into the handle of his Glock .50 and cocked its slide. He looked at Arnez, who discreetly placed his hand on his wrist and shook his head, no. Arnez knew he was about to pop Zekey, and he wasn't trying to have it go down like that. He loved the old nigga to death!

KiMani took a breath and tried to calm himself down. He was just going to make this move with Zekey and get it over with.

Arnez parked three houses down and threw the Tahoe in park. He then turned around in his seat so he could look between KiMani and Zekey while talking to them.

"Look, I'ma let y'all out right here and cut around the corner," Arnez informed them. "Y'all know that alley we passed on our way over here?"

"Yeah." KiMani nodded as he recalled the alley.

"What about it?" Zekey asked.

"Once y'all smoke them fools, make a right and haul ass down the alley," Arnez told them. "I'll be waiting at the end of it for y'all."

Snap! Click! Clack!

The sound of Zekey's Glock being loaded, cocked, and locked with the fifty-round drum resonated inside of the stolen Tahoe.

"Perfect. These fools be serving they shit out the back doe," Zekey said. "Soon as we pop 'em, we'll hop the fence and make our escape."

"Sounds like a plan." Arnez nodded approvingly. He then looked to KiMani, holding out his fist. "Love, foolie."

"Love." KiMani dapped him up.

Arnez made the same exchange with Zekey.

Zekey and KiMani hopped out of the SUV and made their way down the sidewalk. They kept a close eye on their surroundings to make sure there weren't any nosy ass niggaz watching them. The closer they drew to Travieso's grandmother's yard, the louder and clearer the children's voices became. Hunching low, KiMani and Zekey crept up to the driveway and hid behind the Chevy Styleline. KiMani poked his head out, spying on the little girls. They were ignorant to his and Zekey's presence.

"Aye, we gon' creep into the backyard on the opposite side of this car. That way we can avoid the girls seeing us," KiMani informed Zekey of his plan.

Zekey looked on the side of the Chevy Styleline and saw that there wasn't enough room for them to creep alongside it. "Nah." Zekey shook his head, no. "There isn't enough room for us to squeeze past. This nigga parked too close to the goddamn wall," he told him in a hushed tone.

"Okay. Fuck it," KiMani said. "We'll just move past them as quiet as we can. Hopefully, they don't see us. I doubt it, though. It's worth a try."

"Blood, fuck this!" Zekey said loud enough for the girls to hear him. He ran from behind the Chevy Styleline in the direction of the girls. They screamed and cried when they saw him. He looked scary wearing the mask and holding that gun.

"Ahhhh! Ahhhhh! Aaahhhh!" the girls screamed louder and louder.

Zekey snatched up the little girl so fast she dropped her ice cream cone. The front porch light popped on and the front door swung open. A shaved-head Mexican dude wearing a wife beater and tan Dickies stepped out on the porch. He shouted something at Zekey in Spanish and pointed his gun at him. He tried to take a shot at him, but he didn't want to risk hitting the girl. His hesitation gave KiMani, who had run from behind the Chevy Styleline behind Zekey, time to react. The young nigga swung his Glock up and squeezed its trigger. It vibrated in his hand as it spat fire angrily. The Mexican fool hollered out as he took three to the chest and fell against the front door. He slid down to the porch and released his grip on his gun.

"What the fuck are you doing, man?" KiMani screamed out at Zekey as he rushed up the driveway behind him.

"Fuck you think, youngsta? Using this lil' spic bitch as a shield!" Zekey said aloud. He used the screaming little girl as a human shield as he invaded the backyard. "The eses won't be so fast to pop at me when they see I've got one of their own."

Piece of shit, using that lil' girl as a shield! Coldhearted bastard! I swear onna stacka Bibles, I'ma clap his ass after this move, KiMani thought. He invaded the backyard beside Zekey. They ran into two cholos, who happened to be running in their direction. They were dressed in all-black hoodies and gripping Dracos with drums. They went to chop down Zekey and KiMani but hesitated when they saw the little girl. Their reluctance would be their undoing. Zekey and KiMani didn't have such reservations when it came to laying them down. They made quick work of them, cutting them down mercilessly with semi-automatic gunfire.

"Gaaah!" The first cholo went down, agony written across his face.

"Ahhhhh!" the second cholo grimaced.

"Please, please, don't shoot me, man! Please!" a toothless dopefiend pleaded, wearing a beanie and a sweatshirt that was torn at the arm. He interlocked his fingers and dropped down on his knees. Tears formed in his weary eyes as he begged for his life. Having seen the two cholos sanctioned to guard the house chopped up, he knew he was at the masked gunmen's mercy. He just hoped they would have pity on him and spare his life.

"Aaaahhhhh! Aaaaahhhhh!" the little Mexican girl hollered and hollered, displaying her top row of her three missing teeth. Tears poured out the corners of her eyes and encircled her face.

"Travieso, come out here, bitch nigga! Or, I swear 'fore God, I'ma blow this lil' bitch's head off!" Zekey barked furiously at the thick iron door with the peephole and slot in it. For a moment, there was silence, which seemed to anger Zekey further, so he pressed his gun to the girl's temple. "You've got 'til the count of five, puto! One—three—" he purposely skipped a number to let Travieso know that he was as serious as a heart attack about knocking little mama's head off.

"Pinche mayate, that's my cousin!" Travieso yelled out of the slot.

"More reason why you should get cho brown ass out here! Four—" Zekey continued the countdown.

"Okay, all right, I'm coming out!" Travieso blurted out for fear of Zekey murdering his family in cold blood.

KiMani stood by, scanning the area for any threats. He didn't see any. The only one around was the dopefiend who was still down on his knees.

"You, get the fuck outta here!" KiMani commanded him with the motion of his gun.

The dopefiend scrambled to his beatup sneakers and took off running past KiMani.

"Oh, God bless you! God bless you!" The dopefiend disappeared from the backyard.

As soon as the dopefiend had vanished, the iron door popped open. Zekey licked his lips and smiled, victorious. He was finally going to get his chance to squash Travieso like the cockroach he saw him as.

"Alright, I'm coming out, homie, don't shoot," Travieso said.

"Whatever. You just bring yo' ass out here!" Zekey told him.

At this time, the little Mexican girl was whimpering as tears slid down her cheeks.

The iron door opened all the way up, and Travieso slowly stepped out. A frown was etched across his face and he had both his hands up, surrendering. He was a slim Mexican dude who wore his facial hair in a goatee. He had a big shaved head. Unbeknownst to Zekey and KiMani, he was wearing an earbud in his ear. He was also wearing a soft gray hoodie underneath a Pendleton shirt two sizes too big.

"Toss the gun aside, bitch boy!" Zekey ordered.

"You got it, Zekey, just don't hurt her, aye?" Travieso tossed the gun across the yard and put his hands back up in the air.

"What is he saying?" KiMani asked Zekey.

"What chu mean, what is he saying?" a frowning Zekey fired back, but kept his eyes on Travieso.

"Nah, this mothafucka saying something and glancing up at the roof!" KiMani said. He looked up at the roof of the house in time to see two more cholos gripping machine guns, with twin-round drum magazines. Niggaz in the hood referred to their gun as a woman, so they nicknamed the twin-round drum magazines "titties."

"On the roof!" KiMani shouted a warning to Zekey and pointed his gun up at the cholos on the rooftop. He walked backwards as he and Zekey's guns spat flames at them. Each man hollered in agony as they were struck and toppled over. One fell at the bottom of the back porch steps while the other fell flat on his back in front of KiMani. The impact from his fall splattered blood on his murder gear and sneakers.

"Shiesty mothafucka!" Zekey roared heatedly, spit flying off his lips. When the cholos on the rooftop botched their attack, Travieso took advantage of the opportunity and went to grab his gun to save his cousin. "Her blood is on yo' hands—yo' hands!"

When KiMani heard Zekey say this, he looked up to see him pressing his gun to the Mexican girl's head. Right then, everything appeared to be moving in slow motion to him.

"Noooooo!" KiMani screamed and outstretched his hand to stop him. Unfortunately for him, he was far too late. The girl was crying aloud, but she suddenly went silent once Zekey pulled the trigger. Her head burst, splattering blood and brain fragments on his face mask and clothing. He released the limp child's body and it collapsed to the asphalt.

"Fucking pinche, apes, I'll send you both to hell!" a teary-eyed Travieso hollered, seeing his cousin get her head blown off. He came up from the lawn firing his gun at Zekey while retreating towards the gate.

Travieso tucked his gun and leaped upon the gate, scaling it in a hurry. Once he reached the top, he fucked around and lost his bearings, crashing to the ground, hard. He got back up, wincing and running, looking over his shoulder. He could see KiMani and Zekey chasing after him on the opposite side of the gate. That's when he slowed to a stop and pulled his gun back out. Turning around, he extended his piece and fired it vengefully.

Blam, blam, blam, blam!

Sparks flew from off the gate as bullets deflected off it. KiMani and Zekey ducked and scrambled out of the way, trying not to get their heads blown off. Seeing he'd gotten the assassins off his ass for the time being, Travieso started back running, huffing and puffing as he went along. A coat of sweat had formed on his brows, so he wiped it away. When he heard hurried footsteps behind him, he looked over his shoulder again, to see KiMani and Zekey. They'd just run up to the gate and jumped up on it, scaling it. Seeing he had them in his sights, Travieso turned around with his gun again to get off. But Zekey was already halfway over on the other side of the gate, holding on to it with one hand. He pulled his gun from his waistline and pointed it at Travieso, pulling the trigger to keep him at bay.

Bloc, bloc, bloc, bloc!

Travieso backed up, gripped his gun with both hands, and squeezed the trigger.

Blam, blam, blam!

Homeboy continued to blaze at the opposition as he backed away. KiMani and Zekey jumped down from the gate, chasing after Travieso. They brought the firefight to him! The gun battle proved to be too much for Travieso on his own, so he retreated down the alley. He made it out of the alley and had gotten halfway across the street when a Tahoe slammed into him. His body went up on the hood of the massive SUV, rolled down, and smacked against the pavement.

Arnez pulled himself out of the window and sat on its sill. He looked down the alley seeing KiMani and Zekey coming up fast.

"Come on, Blood!" Arnez hollered out and waved them forward. He could hear the police car sirens hastily approaching, and he was trying to get out of there before they arrived.

Arnez slipped back inside of the truck and popped the door locks. KiMani snatched open the backdoor and slid into the backseat. He slammed the door shut behind him. As soon as he did, Zekey was running up. He reached for the handle of the door, but then he stopped. The moaning of Travieso grabbed his attention, and he started his way over to the grill of the Tahoe.

Arnez stuck his head out of the window and hollered at Zekey. "Man, what the fuck you doing? We've gotta get the hell outta here!"

"Shhhhh," Zekey hushed him with his finger to his lips.

"Blood, you won't believe the shit this nigga did back there!"

Zekey overheard KiMani as he walked up on Travieso. He was lying on the ground bleeding at the mouth with his legs and arms at funny angles.

"Aaaaah, my b—back! My back—" Travieso complained, giving glimpses of his bloody teeth. Wincing, he looked ahead to see a masked gunman walking up on him.

"Tu espalda es el menor de tus putos problemas, amigo (Your back is the least of your fucking problems, homeboy)," Zekey told him as he pulled the full-face neoprene mask up to reveal his identity. Travieso's eyes stretched wide open, he gasped, and his heart thudded in a panic.

Zekey pointed his gun down at Travieso's face and sent him to a place where summer never ended. He took his time to admire his handiwork before hopping into the front passenger seat of the Tahoe. The SUV sped off down the street, with police car sirens overwhelming the night.

Tranay Adams

Chapter Thirteen

Arnez pulled up to the rally point and everyone jumped out the Tahoe. He ran from around the SUV, heading over to the trunk of his Chevy Impala. He needed to get the duffle bag containing their change of clothes and the gasoline can to set the G-ride ablaze. While he was occupied doing this, KiMani and Zekey were supposed to be changing out of their clothes.

Zekey sat his gun down on the hood of the Tahoe and pulled his hoodie from over his head. He then started unbuckling his belt and removing his jeans. KiMani came from around the opposite side of the SUV and cracked him in his mouth. Zekey staggered backwards with his jeans around his ankles and fell awkwardly to the ground. He turned over on his elbows and looked at KiMani, blinking his eyes like he'd just awakened.

"I told yo' mothafucking ass before we got there, I'm not slumping any kids, and what the fuck did you do? You killed a poor, defenseless lil' girl," KiMani barked on him.

"Yeah, you're right—I did," Zekey told him as blood slid out the corner of his mouth. He smiled devilishly and wiped his mouth. "Guess what? I'd do that lil' bitch again, if it meant I could get my hands on Travieso."

"You're a diseased dog that has to be put down—for good!" Kimani said, extending his gun to Zekey's forehead. The older man was on his hands and knees, like a dog. He stared up at the youth fearlessly. He wasn't afraid of death. In fact, he welcomed it.

"Oh, yeah? And who's gonna be the one to do it?" Zekey smiled.

"Me!" KiMani snarled and squeezed the trigger.

"Nooooo!" Arnez screamed.

Bloc!

Arnez kicked KiMani's wrist, and his gun discharged close to Zekey's ear. Zekey clutched at the side of his head as an eerie siren wailed within his ear canal. His eyes were bulged and his lips were pursed. He fell several times trying to get back up on his feet. The overwhelming sound of the piece being fired so close to his ear had thrown off his equilibrium. When he finally did make it up on his feet, he was staggering like a drunk out of a bar. He could see Arnez and KiMani arguing and struggling over control of his gun. It appeared like the youngsta was trying to come over and pop his ass, but Arnez was trying to stop him.

Zekey pulled his jeans up and crashed to the ground. He looked to the hood of the Tahoe and spotted his gun. His face transformed to a mask of determination and hatred. His only function now was to pop KiMani for attempting to knock the noodles out of his head. It took several attempts, but Zekey finally managed to grab his blower from off the hood. He turned around, struggling to maintain his balance as well as his aim. That didn't stop him from blasting at KiMani though. The first shot went wild and wasn't nearly as close as Zekey would have liked for it to have been.

The first shot also alerted KiMani and Arnez to the fact that Zekey was strapped. Seeing Zekey was incapable of taking a decent shot, KiMani decided to take advantage of the situation.

"Fuck out my way, Blood!" KiMani shoved Arnez aside roughly. "I'ma put old head outta his misery." He ran forward and got down on one knee, lifting his gun. He angled his head and shut one of his eyes. Arnez was running towards KiMani as fast as he could for fear of him baptizing Zekey in his own blood.

"Ki, no, stop!" Arnez said, drawing closer to him. "Unc, stop! No!"

Bloc! Bloc!

Zekey fired two more shots. One zipped dangerously close to KiMani's head, while the other struck the ground, creating a dirt cloud. KiMani's eyebrows slanted and his nose wrinkled. He'd just lined up the sightings of his gun with Zekey's forehead.

Bloc!

To Be Continued
The Last of the OG's 2
Coming Soon

Submission Guideline

Submit the first three chapters of your completed manuscript to ldpsubmissions@gmail.com, subject line: Your book's title. The manuscript must be in a .doc file and sent as an attachment. Document should be in Times New Roman, double spaced and in size 12 font. Also, provide your synopsis and full contact information. If sending multiple submissions, they must each be in a separate email.

Have a story but no way to send it electronically? You can still submit to LDP/Ca$h Presents. Send in the first three chapters, written or typed, of your completed manuscript to:

LDP: Submissions Dept
Po Box 944
Stockbridge, Ga 30281

DO NOT send original manuscript. Must be a duplicate.
Provide your synopsis and a cover letter containing your full contact information.
Thanks for considering LDP and Ca$h Presents.

Coming Soon from Lock Down Publications/Ca$h Presents

BOW DOWN TO MY GANGSTA

By **Ca$h**

TORN BETWEEN TWO

By **Coffee**

THE STREETS STAINED MY SOUL **II**

By **Marcellus Allen**

BLOOD OF A BOSS **VI**

SHADOWS OF THE GAME II

TRAP BASTARD II

By **Askari**

LOYAL TO THE GAME **IV**

By **T.J. & Jelissa**

IF LOVING YOU IS WRONG... **III**

By **Jelissa**

TRUE SAVAGE **VIII**

MIDNIGHT CARTEL IV

DOPE BOY MAGIC IV

CITY OF KINGZ III

By **Chris Green**

BLAST FOR ME **III**

A SAVAGE DOPEBOY III

CUTTHROAT MAFIA III

DUFFLE BAG CARTEL VI

HEARTLESS GOON VI

By **Ghost**

Tranay Adams

A HUSTLER'S DECEIT III

KILL ZONE **II**

BAE BELONGS TO ME III

A DOPE BOY'S QUEEN III

By **Aryanna**

COKE KINGS V

KING OF THE TRAP II

By **T.J. Edwards**

GORILLAZ IN THE BAY V

3X KRAZY III

De'Kari

THE STREETS ARE CALLING II

Duquie Wilson

KINGPIN KILLAZ IV

STREET KINGS III

PAID IN BLOOD III

CARTEL KILLAZ IV

DOPE GODS III

Hood Rich

SINS OF A HUSTLA II

ASAD

KINGZ OF THE GAME VI

Playa Ray

SLAUGHTER GANG IV

RUTHLESS HEART IV

By Willie Slaughter

THE HEART OF A SAVAGE III

The Last of the OG's

By Jibril Williams

FUK SHYT II

By Blakk Diamond

TRAP QUEEN

By Troublesome

YAYO V

GHOST MOB II

Stilloan Robinson

KINGPIN DREAMS III

By Paper Boi Rari

CREAM II

By Yolanda Moore

SON OF A DOPE FIEND III

By Renta

FOREVER GANGSTA II

GLOCKS ON SATIN SHEETS III

By Adrian Dulan

LOYALTY AIN'T PROMISED III

By Keith Williams

THE PRICE YOU PAY FOR LOVE III

By Destiny Skai

I'M NOTHING WITHOUT HIS LOVE II

SINS OF A THUG II

By Monet Dragun

LIFE OF A SAVAGE IV

MURDA SEASON IV

GANGLAND CARTEL IV

CHI'RAQ GANGSTAS III

By **Romell Tukes**

QUIET MONEY IV

EXTENDED CLIP III

By **Trai'Quan**

THE STREETS MADE ME III

By **Larry D. Wright**

IF YOU CROSS ME ONCE II

ANGEL III

By **Anthony Fields**

FRIEND OR FOE III

By **Mimi**

SAVAGE STORMS III

By **Meesha**

BLOOD ON THE MONEY III

By J-Blunt

THE STREETS WILL NEVER CLOSE II

By K'ajji

NIGHTMARES OF A HUSTLA III

By King Dream

THE WIFEY I USED TO BE II

By Nicole Goosby

IN THE ARM OF HIS BOSS

By Jamila

MONEY, MURDER & MEMORIES III

Malik D. Rice

CONCRETE KILLAZ II

By Kingpen

HARD AND RUTHLESS II

By Von Wiley Hall

LEVELS TO THIS SHYT II

By Ah'Million

MOB TIES II

By SayNoMore

BODYMORE MURDERLAND II

By Delmont Player

THE LAST OF THE OGS II

Tranay Adams

Available Now

RESTRAINING ORDER **I & II**

By **CA$H & Coffee**

LOVE KNOWS NO BOUNDARIES **I II & III**

By **Coffee**

RAISED AS A GOON I, II, III & IV

BRED BY THE SLUMS I, II, III

BLAST FOR ME I & II

ROTTEN TO THE CORE I II III

A BRONX TALE I, II, III

DUFFLE BAG CARTEL I II III IV V

HEARTLESS GOON I II III IV V

A SAVAGE DOPEBOY I II

Tranay Adams

DRUG LORDS I II III
CUTTHROAT MAFIA I II
By **Ghost**
LAY IT DOWN **I & II**
LAST OF A DYING BREED I II
BLOOD STAINS OF A SHOTTA I & II III
By **Jamaica**
LOYAL TO THE GAME I II III
LIFE OF SIN I, II III
By **TJ & Jelissa**
BLOODY COMMAS I & II
SKI MASK CARTEL I II & III
KING OF NEW YORK I II,III IV V
RISE TO POWER I II III
COKE KINGS I II III IV
BORN HEARTLESS I II III IV
KING OF THE TRAP
By **T.J. Edwards**
IF LOVING HIM IS WRONG…I & II
LOVE ME EVEN WHEN IT HURTS I II III
By **Jelissa**
WHEN THE STREETS CLAP BACK I & II III
THE HEART OF A SAVAGE I II
By **Jibril Williams**
A DISTINGUISHED THUG STOLE MY HEART I II & III
LOVE SHOULDN'T HURT I II III IV
RENEGADE BOYS I II III IV

The Last of the OG's

PAID IN KARMA I II III

SAVAGE STORMS I II

By **Meesha**

A GANGSTER'S CODE I &, II III

A GANGSTER'S SYN I II III

THE SAVAGE LIFE I II III

CHAINED TO THE STREETS I II III

BLOOD ON THE MONEY I II

By J-Blunt

PUSH IT TO THE LIMIT

By **Bre' Hayes**

BLOOD OF A BOSS **I, II, III, IV, V**

SHADOWS OF THE GAME

TRAP BASTARD

By **Askari**

THE STREETS BLEED MURDER **I, II & III**

THE HEART OF A GANGSTA I II& III

By **Jerry Jackson**

CUM FOR ME I II III IV V VI

An **LDP Erotica Collaboration**

BRIDE OF A HUSTLA **I II & II**

THE FETTI GIRLS **I, II& III**

CORRUPTED BY A GANGSTA I, II III, IV

BLINDED BY HIS LOVE

THE PRICE YOU PAY FOR LOVE I II

DOPE GIRL MAGIC I II III

By **Destiny Skai**

Tranay Adams

CASH MONEY HO'S
THE WIFEY I USED TO BE
By Nicole Goosby
TRAPHOUSE KING **I II & III**
KINGPIN KILLAZ I II III
STREET KINGS I II
PAID IN BLOOD **I II**
CARTEL KILLAZ I II III
DOPE GODS I II
By **Hood Rich**
LIPSTICK KILLAH **I, II, III**
CRIME OF PASSION I II & III
FRIEND OR FOE I II
By **Mimi**
STEADY MOBBN' **I, II, III**
THE STREETS STAINED MY SOUL
By **Marcellus Allen**
WHO SHOT YA **I, II, III**
SON OF A DOPE FIEND I II
Renta
GORILLAZ IN THE BAY **I II III IV**
TEARS OF A GANGSTA I II
3X KRAZY I II
DE'KARI
TRIGGADALE I II III
Elijah R. Freeman
GOD BLESS THE TRAPPERS I, II, III

The Last of the OG's

THESE SCANDALOUS STREETS I, II, III

FEAR MY GANGSTA I, II, III IV, V

THESE STREETS DON'T LOVE NOBODY I, II

BURY ME A G I, II, III, IV, V

A GANGSTA'S EMPIRE I, II, III, IV

THE DOPEMAN'S BODYGAURD I II

THE REALEST KILLAZ I II III

THE LAST OF THE OGS

Tranay Adams

THE STREETS ARE CALLING

Duquie Wilson

MARRIED TO A BOSS... I II III

By Destiny Skai & Chris Green

KINGZ OF THE GAME I II III IV V

Playa Ray

SLAUGHTER GANG I II III

RUTHLESS HEART I II III

By Willie Slaughter

FUK SHYT

By Blakk Diamond

DON'T F#CK WITH MY HEART I II

By Linnea

ADDICTED TO THE DRAMA I II III

IN THE ARM OF HIS BOSS II

By Jamila

YAYO I II III IV

A SHOOTER'S AMBITION I II

Tranay Adams

By S. Allen

TRAP GOD I II III

By Troublesome

FOREVER GANGSTA

GLOCKS ON SATIN SHEETS I II

By Adrian Dulan

TOE TAGZ I II III

LEVELS TO THIS SHYT

By Ah'Million

KINGPIN DREAMS I II

By Paper Boi Rari

CONFESSIONS OF A GANGSTA I II III

By Nicholas Lock

I'M NOTHING WITHOUT HIS LOVE

SINS OF A THUG

By Monet Dragun

CAUGHT UP IN THE LIFE I II III

By Robert Baptiste

NEW TO THE GAME I II III

MONEY, MURDER & MEMORIES I II

By **Malik D. Rice**

LIFE OF A SAVAGE I II III

A GANGSTA'S QUR'AN I II III

MURDA SEASON I II III

GANGLAND CARTEL I II III

CHI'RAQ GANGSTAS I II

By **Romell Tukes**

The Last of the OG's

LOYALTY AIN'T PROMISED I II

By Keith Williams

QUIET MONEY I II III

THUG LIFE I II

EXTENDED CLIP I II

By **Trai'Quan**

THE STREETS MADE ME I II

By **Larry D. Wright**

THE ULTIMATE SACRIFICE I, II, III, IV, V, VI

KHADIFI

IF YOU CROSS ME ONCE

ANGEL I II

By **Anthony Fields**

THE LIFE OF A HOOD STAR

By Ca$h & Rashia Wilson

THE STREETS WILL NEVER CLOSE

By K'ajji

CREAM

By Yolanda Moore

NIGHTMARES OF A HUSTLA I II

By King Dream

CONCRETE KILLAZ

By Kingpen

HARD AND RUTHLESS

By Von Wiley Hall

GHOST MOB II

Stilloan Robinson

CPSIA information can be obtained
at www.ICGtesting.com
Printed in the USA
LVHW051517190421
684911LV00010B/1261